Dan Headed the "Oriole" for the Harbor.

The Battleship Boys' First Step Upward

OR

Winning Their Grades as Petty Officers

By
FRANK GEE PATCHIN

Illustrated

WILDSIDE PRESS

The Battleship Boys' First Step Upward

CHAPTER I

SIGHTING THE SHOOTING STAR

"GREEN light off the starboard bow, sir."
The voice came from the black void far above the navigating bridge of the battleship "Long Island."

"Where away?" demanded the watch officer on the bridge.

"Two points off starboard bow, sir."

"What do you make her out?"

"Don't make her out, sir," answered the red-haired Sam Hickey, who was doing lookout duty on the platform beside the number one search-light.

"Do you still see her?"

"No, sir."

The watch officer gazed through his night glass in the direction indicated, but was unable to pick up a light of any sort. The "Long Island" was plunging through a great gale, which she was taking head on. White-tipped seas, backed by solid walls of water were sweeping the bridge more than forty feet above the level of the sea. Even the red-haired boy clinging to the rail far above the bridge was now and again nearly swept from his feet by the rush of water that enveloped him.

A sixty-mile gale was sweeping the Atlantic seaboard, with the wind shrieking weirdly through the huge cage masts, whose tops were lost in the darkness above the ship itself. Every man on deck was clinging to stanchion and rail in momentary danger of being swept overboard.

"You must have been mistaken," shouted the watch officer.

"No, sir. It was a light all right, sir," shouted Sam Hickey in a confident tone.

"What did it look like?"

"It looked like a shooting star, sir."

"What was it?"

"It was a shooting star, sir."

A half articulated exclamation of disgust from the officer on the bridge reached the ears of the lookout.

"It shot right up from the sea, sir."

"What's that?"

The question was hurled up at Sam with almost explosive force.

"The star shot right up from the sea, sir."

Now, the watch officer on the bridge of the battleship knew full well that shooting stars shoot downward, not upward. He knew also that with a sky overcast as was this one, with the clouds hanging low, no shooting star could be made out, even granting that one had fallen.

"Boatswain's mate!" roared the officer.

"Aye, aye, sir," answered a hoarse voice somewhere from the depths below.

"Turn out the top watches. Man the tops on the jump!"

"Aye, aye, sir."

Loud words of command floated up from below and a moment later a group of sailors dashed up to the bridge, rubbing their eyes sleepily. Without awaiting a word of instruction, they began running up the iron ladders of the cage masts and were quickly lost to view.

The watch officer raised his megaphone, pointing it up into the air.

"Look sharp two points to starboard. See if you can pick up a light. Keep your eyes open. Boatswain's mate!"

"Aye, aye, sir."

"Station men all the way up the mast to pass the word down in case any lights are made out. I'll never hear the word shouted from up there in this howling gale."

"Aye, aye, sir."

"Green light four points off the starboard bow," howled Sam Hickey.

"Green-light-off-the-starboard-bow," sang a chorus of voices from somewhere far up in the steel mast.

"Man in the top says it's a rocket, sir," was passed down from mouth to mouth.

"Aye, aye, I saw it," answered the watch officer. "Pass the word up to hold the watch. Messenger!"

"Aye, aye, sir."

"Run for the captain's quarters. Tell his orderly we have sighted green rockets off the starboard bow. We have made out no other lights, but there is a ship in trouble off there."

The messenger saluted and was away in a twinkling, racing along the slippery superstructure, guided only by his knowledge of the ship, for he could not see a half dozen feet ahead of him.

The word was passed to the commanding officer by the latter's orderly, and in an incredibly short time the captain emerged from his cabin, fully clothed, his uniform covered by shining black rainclothes.

He quickly made his way to the navigator's bridge, arriving there only a few minutes behind the messenger.

"What's this, Mr. Brant?" he demanded sharply in the ear of the watch officer.

"Signal rockets, sir."

"You are sure of this?"

"Yes, sir. Half a dozen men aloft have sighted them. I saw one flash myself."

"Where away?"

"Four points off the starboard bow the last time we sighted the light, sir."

"How are you heading?"

"East southeast, three quarters, sir."

"Hold the helm steady until we see if we can make out another signal. Up aloft, there!"

"Aye, aye, sir."

"Look sharp for lights. Report them quickly and make sure the word is passed down. Pass the word back after it reaches me, so that you may be sure I have it."

"Aye, aye, sir."

An interval followed, during which only the roar and shriek of the gale were heard. Then all at once the red-haired boy's voice sounded above the storm.

"Shooting star again, three points——"

"What's that?" roared the commanding officer.

"I mean—I mean I sighted the green rocket again, sir," explained Sam Hickey lamely.

"Don't you know——"

"I caught the flash of it, sir," spoke the watch officer. "It was as Seaman Hickey said, three points off the starboard bow this time."

"Starboard, two points!" commanded the captain.

"Starboard two points," repeated the quarter-master on duty at the wheel, giving the steering wheel a sharp turn. "She's on the mark, sir."

"Hold it."

"You think it is a wreck, sir?" questioned the watch officer.

"I know no more about it than do you. Naturally it is some vessel in distress, else they would not be making distress signals. You say you caught only the flash—you did not get a sight of the rocket itself?"

"No, sir. I saw the flash, that was all."

The captain glanced up into the darkness.

"She should be ten miles away, then. We ought to be heading about dead on, if your sight was correct. Full speed ahead, both engines."

The throb of the engines far below them rose to a steady purr. The "Long Island" plunged ahead, lurching more violently than before. It was an unsafe speed in such a sea, but perhaps there were human lives at stake off there in that wild swirl of water, and if so it was the first duty of an American seaman to go to their rescue, however great the peril to himself and crew might be.

"There she goes again," shouted the lookout up by the searchlight.

"I caught it that time. The vessel lies dead ahead. Hold your course, quartermaster."

"Aye, aye, sir."

"Ord'ly, turn out the executive officer. Tell him to order the boat crews and the first and second divisions out. Be quick about it."

"Aye, aye, sir."

Boatswains' whistles trilled faintly from the depths of the battleship; boatswains' mates roared out their commands, piping the men from their sleep, and a few minutes later the superstructure was thronged with half-clad figures. Every man of them was soaked to the skin the instant he reached the deck, but unmindful of this every eye was peering into the black mist ahead, the men anxiously questioning each other as to the cause of their being piped out.

No one seemed to know, but older heads shrewdly suspected that somewhere off ahead was a sister ship in dire distress.

"Boatswain's mate!" again came the warning call of the watch officer.

"Aye, aye, sir."

"Pipe all hands to stations."

Once again whistles trilled. The entire crew of the battleship was being called to stations, for again the commanding officer had seen the warning signals shooting up into the sky. Powerful glasses were being leveled at the black abyss ahead, but as yet the officers, of whom there was now quite a group assembled on the bridge, were unable to make out anything on the sea, save the mountains of water that were leaping toward them.

"We must be nearing the place, Mr. Coates," shouted the captain in the ear of his executive officer. "Keep a sharp lookout now. We don't want to have a collision with an old water-logged hulk in this gale. We should run an excellent chance of going to the bottom ourselves."

"Yes, sir," agreed Mr. Coates, as, raising his megaphone, he warned all lookouts to be on their guard.

Sam Hickey, proud in the consciousness that he had been the first to sight the signals of distress, was scanning the troubled seas with keen eyes, from which now and then he brushed the salt brine with an impatient hand.

"If I could see, I'd see," he complained to himself. "I wonder if they have turned out Dan. He knows where I am anyway. There she blows!" suddenly shouted the red-haired boy.

"He's sighted a whale," laughed a young midshipman.

"What do you mean?" roared the captain.

"Light dead ahead, sir. Rocket again, sir."

"Aye, aye," was the answer from the bridge.

The officers there had plainly seen the signal rocket this time, and the green ball seemed to shoot up into the clouds from directly beneath the bow of the "Long Island." The battleship was at that moment riding a mountainous swell, while the vessel from which the signal had been fired was wallowing in the trough of the sea far below. It seemed as if the battleship must slide down the steep wall of water and crush the vessel laboring in the hollow so far beneath them.

"Port your helm!" commanded the captain. "Slow speed astern, starboard engine. Hold her there!"

"There she is, sir," shouted the executive officer, leveling his night glass on the sea valley.

"What do you make of her?"

"Not much of anything. I see faint lights aboard, but that is all."

"Number one searchlight there," called the captain.

"Aye, aye, sir," answered the sailor in charge of the light.

"Throw a light off the port quarter and see if you can pick up that ship."

"Aye, aye, sir."

An instant later a broad shaft of light pierced the blackness of the night. The beam of light traveled slowly about, finally coming to rest on an object in the sea some distance ahead. On this object the officers focused their night glasses.

"Four-masted schooner, sir," called Sam Hickey from his elevated position beside the searchlight.

"All sticks standing?"

"No, sir."

"No, she has only two poles standing now, sir," spoke up the executive officer. "She seems to be in a bad way."

"Steady her," commanded the captain.

"She's steady," answered the quartermaster at the wheel of the battleship.

"Slow both engines ahead."

The "Long Island" was rolling more heavily than before, now and then giving a violent lurch, forcing every person on deck to cling to whatever support was nearest to him. Otherwise men might have been hurled overboard and lost in the tumbling sea.

By this time the schooner was fairly well outlined by the battleship's searchlight, but the lookouts were unable to make out any signs of life on board the distressed ship. They felt sure, however, that the schooner was on its last legs, and that it was a question of moments, perhaps, before she would take her final plunge.

"All depends upon what she is loaded with, as to how long she lasts," decided the captain of the battleship.

"She is flush with the water," answered the executive officer. "I should say she must be loaded with lumber. She would have been down long ago, otherwise."

"I think you are right, Mr. Coates. Hail them with the megaphone as soon as you think you can make them hear. We are to the windward and your voice should carry."

"Schooner ahoy!" shouted the executive officer.

There was no answering word from the disabled schooner. The distance at which the battleship was compelled to keep for its own safety, to say nothing of the roar of the gale, made communication by word of mouth impossible. At this moment another rocket from the schooner seemed to emphasize the necessity for immediate help.

Turning toward the men assembled on the gun deck, the captain addressed them:

"Battleship crew there! A ship is sinking hard by.

"Volunteers are wanted to man the whaleboats. It is a dangerous mission. All who are willing to volunteer, step forward.''

Every man within hearing distance stepped forward, and a crew was quickly chosen. Sam Hickey and Dan Davis were among the twenty-four men who scrambled into the two boats.

Other sailors took their places by the ropes that controlled the raising and lowering of the life boats. The executive officer, now standing on the superstructure, watching the sea and his own ship, was awaiting the moment when, in his judgment, it would be most safe to launch the whaleboats. Not a man in the two boats spoke even in a whisper. They had cast aside their storm clothes, being clad only in trousers and jumpers.

''Get ready.''

''Toss oars,'' commanded the coxswain of each boat.

Every man raised his oar upright.

''Let go the falls,'' commanded the executive officer.

The two whaleboats struck the sea with a mighty splash.

''Cast off! Go!'' shouted the two coxswains, at which the men fell to their oars with a will. But those in the number two whaleboat either had not been quick enough, or else a wave had caught them unawares. Their frail craft was picked up on the crest of a wave and hurled with mighty force against the side of the ship, the smaller boat instantly going to pieces. In a second, thirteen men were struggling in the boiling sea, fighting desperately for their lives.

CHAPTER II

"NUMBER one whaleboat, there! Go on! You'll be dashed to pieces if you try to rescue them," shouted the executive officer, as the boat holding Dan Davis turned about, bent on rescuing the drowning sailors.

"Cast the life buoys!"

Life rings shot over the side of the battleship, grasped by eager hands, and one by one the unfortunate sailors were pulled on board, some with arms or legs broken from being dashed against the iron sides of the battleship. A quick roll call showed that every one of the boat's crew was accounted for.

Sam Hickey had not been injured.

"Man the cutter with a fresh crew," commanded the captain from the bridge, where he was directing operations.

Sam was the first man to run up the ladder and take his place in the boat. No effort was made to turn him out. Three others, who had been in the unfortunate boat, were close at his heels, while the rest of the crew was made up of fresh volunteers.

"Man the oars more quickly this time,"
shouted the captain from the bridge.

The cutter was swung out and slowly lowered
by the falls. At command the boat was let go,
striking the sloping side of a wave which carried the boat some distance from the ship, so
sure had been the judgment of the executive
officer, who had given the command to let go.

At the command "oars out," the oars were
quickly slipped into place. There was no loss
of time now in obeying orders.

"Give way!" commanded the coxswain, at
which the heavy cutter's bow raised clear of
the sea and the boat began plunging toward the
disabled schooner. The latter lay a long distance from the ship, the battleship's commander
not daring to draw closer for fear of smashing
into the sinking vessel, so strong was the sea.

In the meantime the sailors in whaleboat number one were bending to their task, their boat
drawing slowly toward the distressed ship. It
required heroic effort to drive the boat through
that sea. A greater part of the time the craft
was hidden between the great swells, the powerful searchlight from the battleship being unable to locate them. Then slowly the boat would
rise, dripping, from the sea. It seemed almost
as if the whaleboat were shaking the brine from
her shining sides as she righted herself on the

crest of some great wave, poising there for a few brief seconds, then plunging out of sight.

The whaleboat was the first to reach the lee side of the disabled schooner. The windward side of a ship is the side on which the wind is blowing; the lee side, is the opposite side, and is therefore the more quiet. In a storm a ship is always approached, if possible, on the lee side.

"What ship is that?" called the officer in charge of the small boats.

"The 'Oriole.'"

"Where from?"

"Rio de Janeiro. Cargo of mahogany."

"Pass a line."

A rope shot over the whaleboat and was quickly made secure. Slowly the whaleboat was pulled as close to the schooner as it was safe to go. At the command of the officer in charge, half a dozen sailors climbed up the rope and leaped to the deck of the "Oriole."

Dan Davis was the first man over the rail.

"How many persons have you on board?"

"Twenty men, a woman and a child. The latter are my wife and daughter," the master of the craft informed him.

The woman, lashed to the deck house, was clinging to her child, a girl of some seven years.

Without further questioning, Dan sprang for the deck house, at the same time motioning to

another jackie to come to his assistance. Together they cast off the lashings; and, grasping
the woman and child, led them toward the lee
quarter of the ship.

By this time the cutter also had succeeded
in making its way alongside, and the men of
the crew of the "Oriole" began clambering over
the side of the vessel in the effort to reach the
life boats.

"Stand back, you men!" commanded Dan,
thrusting two sailors aside as they crowded the
woman and the little girl, nearly precipitating
them into the sea.

One of the men attempted to strike the Battleship Boy, and was instantly knocked down
for his pains. A second man came at Dan, but
at that instant the red-haired Sam Hickey was
projected at their very feet, where he had been
thrown by a lurch of the ship as he was clambering over the rail. Sam sprang to his feet
and made short work of the second sailor.

"Help me get the woman and child over,"
shouted Dan.

The woman was first lowered into the boat
by means of ropes; then came the girl. As Dan
lifted her, she laid an arm confidingly about his
neck.

"Please, man, won't you save Tommy?" she
called in his ear.

"Tommy?"

"Yes."

"Where is he?"

"Down in the cabin. Tommy is sick, he is. Please; that's a good man."

"Ahoy, down there, let some one catch the girl when I throw her."

Then, addressing the officer in charge of the boat, he said: "If you don't mind, sir, you need not wait for me. There's someone else below, I hear. I'll go for him and then I'll catch the other lifeboat."

The girl was safely caught, and, acting on Dan's suggestion, the officer ordered the oarsmen to give way together.

"Cutter, wait for me!" cried the lad, dashing along the lee side on his way to the cabin. The master of the "Oriole" had already gone over the side, and was now on the way toward the battleship, with his wife and daughter and nearly a dozen exhausted sailors from the schooner. Unfortunately for Dan, the officer in charge of the cutter did not hear Dan's shout, but a few moments later gave the command to return to the battleship, Sam being in the boat.

"Hello, Tom!" shouted Dan, half running, half falling down the companion way into the main corridor of the schooner's cabin.

He stumbled into water that reached above his knees.

"Tom! Tom!" he cried.

There was no response. Dan dived into the little cuddy. The cuddy lamp was burning, swaying widely with each roll of the ship, shedding a faint light over the stuffy room, for everything had been closed up tightly to keep the water that was now everywhere in the ship from drowning out the master's quarters.

A sewing basket, with a half-completed piece of work beside it, lay on the table, while two bunches of bananas hung suspended from the rudder casing.

Dan Davis was dimly conscious of observing all these peaceful signs, though his mind was upon other things.

Once more he raised his voice.

"Tom!" he shouted with all the strength of his lusty lungs.

"Git out, you lubber!"

Dan actually jumped. The voice had seemed to be right at his ear. The voice was hoarse and jeering. The Battleship Boy glanced about him quickly, but could see nothing that looked like a human being.

"That you, Tom?" he demanded.

A shriek of wild laughter was the answer to his question.

Glancing up among the beams, Dan Davis gave a gasp. He understood.

"A parrot! Hello, Tom, is that your name?" he questioned.

The parrot laughed shrilly.

"So you are the Tom I came down here to rescue, are you? Well, this is a nice kettle of lobster! But you shall be rescued, just the same, Mr. Thomas—Mr. Thomas, what's your other name?"

"Lubber," answered the bird of brilliant plumage.

Dan grabbed the cage. Searching hastily about, he found a skirt, which he bound about the cage, knowing that the bird would surely be drowned on the journey to the ship unless the cage were well protected. Tom protested by sundry screeches and unseemly language, to all of which Dan gave no heed.

"We must get out of here. The boat will get tired of waiting for us, and we're not going to stay here and drown," said Dan.

The lad, having bound the cage to his satisfaction, ran up the companionway. As he reached the deck a great wall of water swept over him, a ton or more of it pouring down the open hatchway ere he could get it closed. For a moment he held on desperately, unable to see or hear, for the water that enveloped him.

The wave passed and Dan staggered toward the stern, holding to the rail that was now half submerged under a foaming sea.

"Lifeboat, there!" he called as he neared the stern.

There was no response to his summons. Dan repeated his call, but his voice sounded weak and feeble in the roar of the storm. At last he reached the stern and, during a lull in the rush of water, peered over. The cutter was not there. Running to the other side, he looked over, but he saw nothing but a waste of tumbling sea.

For a moment the Battleship Boy stood clinging to the rail in a dazed sort of a way. Then the truth dawned upon him.

"They have gone back to the ship without me," he groaned. "I have been left on a sinking ship. Even if they discover my absence it will no doubt be too late to come to my rescue before this old tub goes down. Tom Lubber, it begins to look as if you and I were bound for Davy Jones's Locker at a twenty-knot gait."

"Git out," jeered the parrot.

CHAPTER III

BOMBARDED BY BIG GUNS

DAN was cool under the dreadful situation in which he found himself. His mind was clear and active now. He felt no sense of fear.

Glancing about, he finally located the battleship, though he was able to see it only when the schooner rose on some mighty swell. The ship appeared to be far away, but from her forward cage mast a broad beam of light was being thrown down on the water. After a time Dan made out a speck on the water near the warship.

"That's the cutter," he muttered. "Thank goodness, they have not been swamped. I wonder what became of the other boat? They must have gotten aboard before this. But how came the cutter to go away and leave me so soon, I cannot understand."

Dan did not know that his warning to the cutter to wait for him had not been heard by the coxswain of the latter boat, the lifeboat having pulled away almost at once. The lad now shouted at the top of his voice, but he could not have been heard a ship's length away.

Once the big searchlight fell across the wave-swept decks of the "Oriole," hovered there a moment, then was quickly withdrawn.

"The boats are safe on board, I guess," decided Dan. "The ship is moving. They are going away. I am left. I guess I had better go below or I shall be swept into the sea. As it is, I shall not have very long to wait for the end, judging from the way the schooner is listing. "Good-bye, old 'Long Island,'" muttered the boy, saluting, as he fixed his eyes on the spot where he figured the stern of the battle-ship should be. Then all was shut out in a blinding wave that swept the deck of the disabled craft.

When the wave had passed, Dan was gripping the deck house, gasping, for he was almost choking with the salt water he had swallowed. He was still clinging to the bird.

"Come, Tom, we had better go below," he said, quickly raising the hatch, letting it fall over him with a bang as he leaped down into the corridor that led to the cuddy. But, quick as he was, a flood of salt water poured down with him. For a moment Dan seemed to be swimming in it.

"Tom Lubber, it strikes me that the safest place for you, just now, will be in your old billet up there. If you are going to be saved, I guess some one else will have to do it. I do not seem to be an entire success as a life saver.''

The bird-cage was placed on its hook, after which the lad stripped the covering from it, bringing from the parrot a chorus of protests and scornful epithets.

Dan curled up on a bunk, leaning against a bulk-head. He was dripping wet, but to this he gave no thought. He did not even realize that such was the case. He was wondering how long it would be ere the old schooner would take a plunge to the bottom of the ocean.

''It must be a long way to the bottom,'' decided the Battleship Boy. ''I shan't know when we reach there, anyway, so what's the odds how far it is? Perhaps it would be better for me to jump overboard and put a quick end to it. Yet,'' he reflected, ''while I am alive I am alive. I guess that's good sense, and it gives me an idea.''

For several moments the boy was lost in deep thought.

''If the rudder is still in place I may be able to do something that will ease matters a little. Of course I do not know how much water there is in the hold. Perhaps the bottom has been burst open, and all that is keeping us together is the lumber. I'm going to make an investigation, at any rate. I wonder if they have discovered my absence on board the battleship?"

* * * * * * * *

They had not discovered his absence. In boarding the battleship with the rescued crew the whaleboat had been wrecked, as had its mate in starting out. One of the rescued men was drowned in the sea just as he was reaching for a rope that had been cast to him by a sailor on the deck of the warship.

For a time there was great excitement on board the battleship. At last, however, all hands were hauled aboard. The cutter's crew and passengers were landed without disaster, the daughter of the master of the "Oriole" looking upon the whole affair as a most delightful experience.

After the rescued sailors had been cared for by their comrades on the battleship, and the master's family made comfortable in one of the cabins of the captain, the latter made his way to the bridge.

"Let us get under way now, Coates," said the captain, addressing the executive officer. "I don't like to lie near that floating hulk there any longer than I am obliged to."

The ship began to move.

"I'll tell you what, Coates, I believe we had better break her up, don't you?"

"The schooner, sir?"

"Yes."

"An excellent idea. Shall I do it?"

"Yes. Use the seven-inch port battery."

"Boatswain's mate!" roared the executive officer.

"Aye, aye, sir."

"Turn out the seven-inch starboard gun crews. Order them to take their stations and stand ready with six rounds of solid shot."

"Aye, aye, sir."

The orders were quickly transmitted to the gun crews by the mate. The men went to their stations on a run. This was an opportunity that delighted the hearts of every jackie on board. It was something more than the ordinary target practice. It was, in reality, battle practice. Ammunition was quickly hoisted to the seven-inch gun turret, and, taking a wide circle, the ship began swinging back toward the spot where the "Oriole" had last been seen. The searchlights were playing over the mountainous seas in search of her.

"There she is, four points off the starboard bow, sir," shouted a lookout.

"What is the range, Mr. Coates?" asked the captain.

"About four thousand yards."

"Better make it three."

The outlines of the schooner could be faintly made out by focusing the searchlight upon her.

"Within the range, sir."

"Very well, when you are ready."

A bell buzzed in the starboard seven-inch forward turret, while an indicator told the waiting gun crew that the doomed ship lay three thousand yards from them. An instant later a projectile had been shoved into the big gun, the breech closed and the gun pointer crawling to his station, was sighting the piece on the ghostly outline of the "Oriole."

"Fire!"

The battleship heeled ever so little, followed by a report as if the ship had blown up.

Again the bell in the turret buzzed.

"Aye, aye, sir," answered the gun captain.

"An excellent shot," came the information in the voice of the executive officer. "You shot away the foremast. The schooner lies very low in the water. You will have to depress your gun a little more this time, or wait until the target rises on a swell. Drill her this time."

"Aye, aye, sir; we'll drill her."

"Boom!" roared the big seven-inch, as it hurled the second heavy projectile straight at the unfortunate schooner.

"Fair hit," shouted the executive officer in a tone of exultation.

"Hit her hard, sir?"

"Dead amidships. Smash another in the same place and you'll have her on the way to Davy Jones's ditty box."

Again the forward starboard seven-inch spoke.

"Miss," came the warning. "Poor work. Cease firing and give the after turret's crew a chance."

"Aye, aye, sir."

The after-turret's crew sprang to their work with a shout of joy. In an incredibly short time after receiving the command, their weapon began to roar, shot following shot, as if they were engaged in record target practice for the silver cup.

"Hit," came the call down the speaking tube after each shot. Projectile after projectile landed in the hull of the doomed schooner.

"There she goes!" cried the captain, catching a faint glimpse of the "Oriole" as she slipped down a great sloping hill of water. "That's the last of her."

"Shall we give her another round, sir?"

"No; cease firing. She is no doubt broken to pieces by our shot by this time. You do not see her, do you?"

"No, sir. The searchlight doesn't seem able to find the schooner."

"Then we need trouble ourselves no further about her. It's a good job, Coates," smiled the captain, rubbing his palms together in keen satisfaction. "We have rescued the crew of a disabled ship in one of the worst gales that I ever saw on the Atlantic coast. We have lost none of our own men and only one of the seamen belonging to the schooner. Of course I'm sorry that he was lost, but we did all that human beings could accomplish."

"We did, sir."

At that moment the captain's orderly approached.

"What is it?" demanded the captain, observing that the orderly wished to say something to him.

"Seaman Sam Hickey asks permission to speak to the commanding officer, sir."

"What does Seaman Hickey wish to say to me?"

"He did not say, sir."

"I will see him."

Sam, his red hair standing straight up, for he was hatless as well as coatless still, approached the captain, came to attention and saluted.

"Well, lad, what is it?"

"I have not seen my friend Dan Davis since the boats returned, sir," he said.

"What's that?"

"I find that Davis did not return in either the whaleboat or the cutter. He went back to save some one that the girl begged him to save. I've made inquiry and learn that the somebody was a miserable parrot."

"Seaman Davis on that schooner?" demanded the captain in a startled voice.

"Yes, sir, I think so, sir."

"And we have shot the decks from under him with our seven-inch guns!" groaned the captain.

He immediately ordered that the searchlights try again to pick the schooner up. But no search revealed her. By reason of the violence of the gale, the battleship, for her own safety, had been compelled to steam some distance away. But she lay to throughout the night, and only when the early daylight revealed nothing of the schooner was she headed for the Delaware Breakwater.

CHAPTER IV

WE left Dan curled up in a bunk, wondering how long it would be before the schooner would go to the bottom.

"What's that?" exclaimed Dan, starting up from the narrow berth on which he was sitting.

He had heard a crash and felt a jar that was different from the shocks he had been experiencing for the last half hour.

Suddenly the Battleship Boy leaped from the berth, splashing into the water knee deep, as another shock, more violent than the other, set the doomed schooner trembling from stem to stern.

"Another mast has gone by the board," he groaned.

"Bang!"

The sound was accompanied by a ripping and rending of woodwork as if the vessel were being torn apart by some strange, wonderful power.

"I can't stand this any longer. I've got to go on deck and find out what is occurring, even if I am swept overboard. I'm not going to die down in this hole anyway. It's no way for a

jackie in Uncle Sam's Navy to end his life.
Tommy, you'll have to get along the best way
you can. Good-bye if I do not see you again,"

There was a note of regret in the Battleship
Boy's tone, as his glance lingered half regret-
fully on the ugly face of the parrot.

"Lubber!" retorted the indignant parrot.

"I guess I am all you accuse me of being,"
answered Dan with a mirthless laugh.

Running up the companionway he crouched
under the hatchway, listening in order to determine whether a wave were washing over the
ship or just leaving the stern. Having decided
on this, the lad quickly threw open the hatch
and sprank out on deck.

A cold blast of salt spray smote him full in
the face. Dan cleared his eyes and glanced
about him inquiringly. He was able to see but
little of deck or mast, but he felt quite sure
that only one of the latter had been left standing.

There was a sudden angry flash off to port.

"Lightning," muttered Dan. "We're going
to have a thunderstorm to add to my other
troubles."

No sooner were the words out of his mouth
than the ship received a shock so sudden and
violent as to throw the boy flat on his face on
the deck.

"That's the time we were struck," he cried, springing up.

Indeed the "Oriole" had been struck, but not in the way that Dan Davis thought. Instead of being struck by lightning another projectile from the seven-inch gun had torn its way through the stricken schooner.

Dan never had been under fire; in fact, he never had taken part in target practice, so he knew little of what big-gun fire was like.

A beam from a searchlight smote his face.

"The 'Long Island'!" he fairly shouted. "They're coming back for me. Tom," he yelled, poking his head in through the hatchway, "they're coming after us. We shall yet be saved."

"Get out!" answered the parrot in a shrill screaming voice.

Dan dropped the hatchway, straightened up and shading his eyes as he gazed off across the waste of waters. Just then he caught sight of another of those sharp flashes that he had taken for lightning. This time he saw that the flash had come directly from the battleship itself. At the same instant he experienced another of those terrific shocks, this one sending him staggering to the rail.

The truth suddenly dawned upon him.

"They are shooting at me!' he gasped. "But why are they doing that terrible thing?"

Dan pondered over this for a full moment.

"I know," he cried. "They are trying to sink the schooner, to get her out of the way, so that no other ship will run into her in the darkness. Well, I certainly am in a fine fix. Not being able to drown myself in a respectable way, the ship has come to my help by shooting at me. I wonder what gun they are doing it with? It must be the twelve-inch, judging——"

"Bang! Crash!"

"There she goes again."

The schooner heeled until the lad was sure that she was going to turn turtle. The Battleship Boy felt a shiver running up and down his spine.

"If I had a light I might signal them and attract their attention. I don't believe they are able to pick me up with the searchlight. If they saw me they surely would not keep on shooting at me."

Dan hastened to the cabin below. There was not a lantern to be found so he grabbed up the cuddy lamp and ran to the deck with it. The instant he reached the deck the wind blew the light out.

The boy put the lamp down on the deck and

crept over to the port rail which was the side
nearest to the distant battleship.

Once more the seven-inch gun let go, the projectile going just a little high and cutting a gash
in the deck as it went screaming over, losing itself in the sea off to starboard somewhere.

"About six feet nearer, and my name would
have been Dennis," muttered the lad.

He remembered, afterwards, that he had not
experienced any feeling of fear. The sensation
of being under fire, and that with the knowledge
that a battleship was trying to sink the vessel
under him, filled him with awe and curiosity.
Dan found himself wondering just how long it
would take for the guns of the warship to put
the schooner under. Had she not been loaded
with lumber the schooner no doubt would have
gone down under the first projectile that struck
her.

"My, but those boys can shoot," he muttered
with a feeling of pride. "Ah, that one went too
high. Lower, lower!" fairly screamed the boy.

"Crash!"

"That's the time you did it," he shouted ex-
ultantly, picking himself up from the deck, his
clothing torn, his body scratched from the splint-
ers that the projectile had rained over him in a
perfect shower. "A few more shots like that
and you'll have her. But I'm glad there isn't

any flag flying here. I'd have to take it down.
I couldn't stand it to see them shooting at the
Stars and Stripes.''

The next shot tore away a large section of the
rail on the port side, and seemed at the same
time to have twisted the ship about.

But Dan was clinging to a stanchion, which
fact saved him from being again thrown to the
deck.

"I guess they must have decided to cease firing," he said. "I hope they haven't given it up.
I know I shall be disappointed. How I wish I
were at that gun! Wouldn't it be fun! I believe I could shoot as straight as they do.
But——"

Dan did not finish the sentence. There came
a report more terrific than those that had pre-
ceded it. The stanchion to which the lad had
been clinging suddenly doubled over, striking
him on the head, felling him to the deck. The
schooner lurched heavily, and, settling over on
her starboard side, slipped slowly down a great
sloping hill of water into a deep hollow of the
sea. But Dan Davis lay still. The blow on his
head had been a cruel one, the iron stanchion
having been struck by a projectile from one of
the seven-inch guns and bent double.

The first gray streaks of the dawn were shooting up from the angry sea when Dan opened

his eyes again. His first sensation was that of
choking. He was, indeed, choking, for the deck
on which he lay was a river of salt water. The
lad, in falling, had become wedged between the
rails, this being the only thing that had kept
him from being washed overboard.

The lad's first thought was that he was drowning. Soon, however, he managed to get his eyes
open sufficiently to examine his surroundings.

There was gray, turbulent water wherever the
eye roamed, a waste of foaming sea, here and
there heaping itself into great dark piles that
seemed to tower higher than the masts of a ship.

"It's a wonder I'm alive," exclaimed the Battleship Boy, as he began extricating himself
from his uncomfortable position. "The sea is
not nearly so high as it was last night, and this
old craft is still on its legs. That is the most
surprising thing about the whole business."

Dan got to his feet, but he was very unsteady.
His first business was to look over the ship and
make up his mind how badly she had been hurt
by the fire of the battleship. Wreck and ruin
greeted him on every hand. The decks were a
mass of tangled wreckage, broken masts, twisted
stanchions and knotted ropes. In several places
the decks were ripped wide open, the lumber
beneath them split and torn into shreds.

Peering over the side, the lad discovered a

jagged hole in the hull, through which the water rushed with every roll of the ship.

The "Oriole" was lying well over on her side, threatening every instant to complete the job by turning over entirely. Dan surveyed the ship with critical eyes.

"I see now what has saved me. It is the lumber. The schooner was so far down in the sea, too, that the shots from the battleship could do her little serious damage. I wonder why they ceased firing. They must have thought we were sinking. Well, anyway, I'm still afloat. I wish I could see the sun so I could guess where I am."

Dan consulted the compass critically, learning that the battered hulk was headed southeast. He tried the steering wheel, making the discovery that the ship's rudder had not been torn off. He uttered an exclamation.

"I wonder if I could do it?" he muttered. "The land lies somewhere to the southwest. I know we are not far from the coast, for we sighted a lighthouse yesterday afternoon."

The stump of a mast was still standing, the stick having broken off about thirty feet from the deck.

Dan, after a moment's reflection, ran below. Wading about in the cuddy and storeroom in water up to his armpits, he found that of which he was in search. He staggered to the deck, dragging a jib sail after him. It was no slight effort to carry the heavy canvas, but the lad accomplished it.

Now his purpose became evident. After great exertion he managed to climb the slippery mast, carrying a block and tackle with him. The roll of the ship made his task doubly difficult, but Dan pluckily held on, weak and lame as he was. He knew no such word as "fail." When he set about a certain task he did so with perfect confidence in himself. He knew he should succeed.

"There. I'm not a half-bad sailor, after all," he cried, dropping to the deck.

His next duty was to carry a rope from the sail that he had fastened to the stump of the mast, back to the steering wheel, first having passed the rope through tackle that he had made secure to a stanchion. Taking it all in all, he had accomplished something that would have been a credit to a much more experienced seaman.

But Dan had not quite finished with his preparations. He was eyeing the heavy mast that lay lengthwise of the deck, amidst a tangled mass of ropes and stays.

Procuring an axe from the deck house he cut the mast free; then, rigging some tackle, he worked with the stick until at last he had dumped it over the stern into the sea. Before doing so,

however, he had made fast a line to it, securing
the line at the stern of the schooner before
launching the spar. The "Oriole" steadied considerably under the influence of the dragging
spar.

"Now, for the experiment!" cried Dan almost joyously. "I don't know, but perhaps the
minute I get some wind in the sail the whole out-
fit will turn turtle. At least, that will be better
than waiting for the ship to do so of her own
accord."

He drew the sail taut, after a long, comprehensive glance over the deck, at the same time
crowding the wheel over to port. Then followed
a minute of anxious suspense. The sail slowly
filled, the shattered bow gradually swung about.
With a "splash, splash, splash!" the battered
hulk of the wrecked, shot-riddled "Oriole" began to move.

"Hip, hip, hurrah!" shouted Dan Davis.
"Right side up with care! Now, if we don't get
any worse weather, we'll land somewhere, even
if it's on the rocks."

Dan decided upon the course that he would
follow if he could, and, watching the compass,
held the "Oriole" to that course as closely as
possible.

All during that day the sea continued gray
and angry, the clouds hung low and the sea gulls

swept screaming by him, bound for still water.
Dan remained steadfast to his vigil, watching
sea and sky and sail with keen, observant eyes.
He could not tell how fast he was traveling, but
so long as the schooner was under motion he did
not care particularly. There was no sight of
land, but still he might be within three or four
miles of the coast and yet be unable to sight it,
for the "Oriole" was low in the water.

Now and then, as the schooner rose on a swell,
he would catch sight of a wisp of smoke on the
far-off horizon, showing that steamers were
working their way up or down the coast.

Dan began to feel faint and hungry. He decided to look for food. Lashing the wheel he
went below and began his search in the dark,
water-logged interior of the ship.

"Git out!" shrieked the parrot.

"I'm going to, just as soon as I find a
cracker."

The parrot shrieked with rage, which caused
the Battleship Boy to laugh almost happily.

After some searching about the lad came upon
a tin case of hard tack that had not been water-
soaked. A piece of this he gave to the parrot,
the rest being stuffed into his own pockets.
Then Dan returned to his wheel.

It was late that afternoon when the lad caught
sight of something ahead in the distance that

attracted his attention instantly. He sprang up to the broken rail, and, supporting himself by a twisted stanchion, peered into the midst of the spray.

"Land ho!" he shouted. "I think I see a light house."

Dan danced about the deck gleefully, for a moment, then grabbed the wheel.

"Gid-dap! You're a slow old poke," he jeered.

After a time he was able to make out the beacon more clearly.

"Somehow, that light house looks familiar to me," he muttered. "I know I have seen it before. Why, of course; I know where I am now. Hurrah! We're headed for the Delaware Breakwater. If I keep on in this way I'll be in Philadelphia—in the course of time," he added with a broad grin.

As Dan Davis and his derelict craft drew nearer and nearer he discovered something else that caused him to gaze fixedly. What he saw was the towering cage masts of a battleship.

"Saved!" cried the Battleship Boy. "And it's the 'Long Island.' I know it is. Won't they be surprised to see me, though? They must have gone in there to get out of the gale."

The lad was swelling with pride. He had accomplished a great feat, and he knew it.

By this time glasses from the warship were being leveled at the strange craft that was to be seen floundering through the sea, headed for the harbor where the battleship was at anchor.

The officer of the deck sent word to the captain, who was below, and the captain, after one look at the wreck approaching, sent for the executive officer.

"What do you make of her, Mr. Coates?" he questioned.

The executive officer took a long, searching look at the schooner, then turned wonderingly toward his superior.

"It's our schooner 'Oriole,' unless I am greatly mistaken, sir."

"You don't mean it?"

"I may be mistaken, but it looks very much like her."

"But we smashed the hulk of the 'Oriole,' Mr. Coates. We saw her go under."

"If we did she has pulled herself together and come back from Davy Jones's Locker to a certainty. There's a man at the wheel, sir. I believe that is Seaman Davis."

"Send a boat's crew out to meet her at once."

A cutter was quickly launched. By this time the rails of the battleship were crowded with jackies. The word had been passed around that the strange craft was none other than the schooner that officers and crew supposed they had broken to pieces in the gale the night before.

Officers, through their glasses, saw the cutter run alongside the schooner. Then, with the lone mariner on board, they began the return trip to the battleship. The cutter came alongside, a few minutes later, and Seaman Daniel Davis ran up the sea ladder, leaped through the rope railing and came to attention before the commander of the battleship.

The instant his salute was returned, Dan ran to the port side of the after deck, where stood a child, clinging to its mother's hand.

"Young lady," he said, "I've brought your parrot to you. But I must say he has about the worst disposition of any parrot that I ever knew."

Dan handed the parrot over to the eager hands of the child.

"Lubber!" shrieked the parrot, making a vicious grab for the Battleship Boy's hand.

The jackies of the "Long Island" set up a mighty cheer that was heard far off on the mainland, wafted there by the quarter gale that was still blowing. At the same time one by one the officers strode forward, grasping the hand of the plucky lad, showering him with congratulations. Dan Davis had performed a feat that would be talked of on shore as well as on the high seas for a long time to come.

"Ord'ly," called the captain sharply.

"Aye, aye, sir."

"Tell the master-at-arms to see to it that Seaman Davis gets a warm meal, the best that the ship affords, and at once. Davis, you will draw a suit of clothes from the canteen at my expense. Yours are ruined. After that you will turn in and stay there till to-morrow morning."

Dan saluted gravely.

As the hulk of the "Oriole" would be dangerous to navigation, she was towed within the Delaware Breakwater and delivered to the proper authorities, and the passengers and crew of the ill-starred schooner went ashore.

CHAPTER V

THAT night being Saturday the crew gave a banquet in honor of the Battleship Boy, following it with an entertainment. There were songs, buck and wing dancing, a little playlet and a lively boxing bout.

Dan was dragged to the stage amid loud demands for a speech.

"Tell us how you did it," shouted the jackies. "Tell us all about it."

The Battleship Boy blushed furiously.

"Mates, I can't do it. I—I——" then Dan fled. They found him, an hour later, hiding in the twelve-inch gun turret.

The officers, however, felt a keen professional interest in the lad's accomplishment, and especially in the effect on the schooner of the big gun-fire. Hardly a man of all that crew of eight hundred men and officers ever had stood on the deck of a ship that was being bombarded by heavy projectiles.

Dan was summoned to the captain's quarters. There, in the presence of the senior officers, he related in a clear, comprehensive manner all that had occurred, describing in detail the shock

when the projectiles hit the schooner; giving
as nearly as possible the degree of list that had
followed and the number of hits. His technical
knowledge was a surprise to the ship's officers.
Such knowledge was unusual in a seaman, showing, as it did, that the lad had used his eyes and
his brain to good purpose since he had been on
shipboard. As a matter of fact, Dan had been
studying ever since his enlistment. He had spent
all his leisure moments in studying the technical works with which the ship's library was
equipped, asking questions of the petty officers,
until he had informed himself far beyond his
grade.

Both lads had by this time risen to the grade
of full seamen, which carried with it a substan-
tial increase in pay.

"What, in your opinion, prevented our fire
from sinking the schooner?" questioned the
captain.

"Why, the fact that the boat was loaded with
lumber was all that kept her afloat, sir. Then,
again, her hull lay so low in the water that the
projectiles had no opportunity to do effective
work. If you had elevated the seven-inch and
dropped a projectile or so on the deck of the
schooner, I might not have been here to tell you
about what happened," added Dan with a sug-
gestive smile.

The captain smiled at his executive officer.

"That is most excellent logic, Mr. Coates."

"Yes, sir."

"I think we shall have to make a full report of this to the Navy Department. Prepare a statement from what Seaman Davis has told us, together with any further technical information he may be able to give you. At the same time full credit should be given to Seaman Davis for his splendid work. Young man, I congratulate you. You are not unknown to me. I well recall other fine deeds on your part performed some time since. I trust you suffered no injury during your trying experience."

"No, sir."

"You are interested in guns?"

"Very deeply interested."

"But you have not been stationed at one of the guns?"

"No, sir."

"Would you like to be? Would you prefer to be a member of a gun crew?"

"It has been my ambition to join a gun crew, sir. I feel that I should do well in that position."

"Then you shall. Coates, will you be good enough to tell the ship's writer to enter Seaman Davis as a member of the starboard seven-inch crew?"

"Yes, sir."

"Thank you, sir," answered the Battleship
Boy, his eyes gleaming with pleasure. "I shall
try not to be a discredit to the seven-inch, sir."

"You will not. That goes without saying."

"May I ask a favor, sir?"

"Certainly. What is it?"

"Will it be possible for my friend, Seaman
Hickey, to have a place in that gun squad?"

"I think that can be arranged," answered the
captain with an indulgent smile. "Has your
friend also a desire to learn to shoot?"

"Yes, sir."

"His desire shall be gratified. And, as for
you, Davis, continue in the way you have started
and there is little doubt as to where you will
eventually bring up. I shall watch your career
with deep interest. I always take an interest in
the young men who are striving to work themselves up. If I can be of assistance to you, at
any time, communicate in the proper manner,
and I shall be glad to do all I can for you."

Dan rose, for they had invited him to be seated
when he first entered the cabin. He came to
stiff attention, saluted and, when the commanding officer waved his hand, the Battleship Boy
executed a smart right-about-face and marched
from the room.

On the following morning Dan and Sam were

marched to the quarter-deck with the seven-inch starboard gun crew at muster. They were proud boys, too, and, after quarters, they proceeded directly to their station, where they spent the forenoon receiving instruction under the captain of the gun's crew.

Dan fondled the great gun almost affectionately. It already had become a thing of life to him, for had not this same gun been thundering away at him, hurling projectiles at him in a determined effort to sink the ship under him, only a few hours before?

"Rather be at this end than the other, wouldn't you?" questioned Sam Hickey, with a grin.

"Yes; now that I have had time to think the matter over, I believe I prefer this end," laughed Dan. "It was not so bad, though. You see, I never had been under fire before, and I was interested. It was a new experience."

"One that few of us have had," spoke up the gun captain.

"I know I should have run away if I had been there," decided Sam, with a thoughtful shake of the head.

"Where would you have run to?" demanded Dan, at which there was a laugh all around.

Sam was sitting on the deck of the turret, industriously at work polishing the brass tompion with which the end of the gun is plugged to keep out the sea water.

Finishing his task, he turned up the tompion and sat down on it, as with chin in hands he listened to the conversation.

"Makes a good seat, eh?" he grinned, as he saw the eyes of the gun captain upon him.

"You will not think so if you damage the tompion. Get off from it. Do you know what those things are worth?"

" 'Bout a dollar and a half," answered Sam rather contemptuously. "I could buy enough to fit the ship with on a month's pay."

"You could, eh?"

"Yes."

"You will have a chance to buy one if you are not careful. Those tompions cost twenty-five dollars apiece, and I ought to know, for I dropped one overboard once and it was checked up against me."

Sam uttered a low whistle of surprise, then very gingerly carried the brass plug outside and inserted it in the muzzle of the big gun. As he did so Sam half turned his head, finding himself looking into the eyes of a dark-faced fellow, who was lounging against the rail.

"Hello, Blackie," greeted the red-haired boy.

The dark-faced boy scowled. He was one of two Hawaiians who had joined the ship about

the same time that the Battleship Boys had
come aboard. One of the Hawaiians was very
dark and the other almost white, so the jackies
named them Black and White, these names
being easier of pronunciation than were the
real names of the men.

As it chanced, both Black and White had
been shifted from the seven-inch gun crew to
make room for Dan and Sam, while the Pacific
Islanders were set to scrubbing decks and doing
general work about the ship.

The men did not dare rebel, but they had been
ugly ever since the change had been made, and
Sam's grin did not tend to make Black any
the less ugly.

"I said 'hello,' " repeated Sam.

Still the Hawaiian made no reply. He simply
scowled—scowled until his face was ridged with
sharp wrinkles.

"Don't you know how to salute, my man?"
urged Sam, with the superior air that he had
seen some officers employ.

"Me know."

"Then salute your superior."

"No salute you. You nothing but red-head."

"Oh, that's it, is it? Because I'm a red-head
you won't salute me? Well, let me tell you,
I had a sight rather have a red head than some
other colors that I know about."

Sam turned on his heel and strode into the gun turret without another word. He did not realize that he had made an enemy of the dark-skinned Hawaiian, an enemy who would never forget to do him an injury. Perhaps Sam would not have cared had he known.

A few moments later the gun captain emerged from the turret and stood leaning over the rail of the ship, looking into the water, one hand resting lightly on the muzzle of the seven-inch gun. Suddenly his hand slipped and went right into the muzzle.

The gun captain withdrew the hand with a surprised look on his face.

"What's this?" he muttered. "What did that red-head do with the tompion, I wonder?"

He glanced about the deck, and, failing to discover the brass gun plug, hurriedly entered the turret where Sam was now engaged in polishing the bright work on the gun butt.

"Hickey!"

"Yes, sir."

"What did you do with that tompion after you polished it?"

"The plug, you mean?"

"Yes."

"Why, I put it back where it belongs."

"Where, I asked you?"

"I stuck it in the gun."

"Come out here."

The gun captain led Sam to the outer deck, and, taking hold of the boy's arm, pointed to the muzzle of the seven-inch.

"Do you see any tompion in that gun?" he demanded.

"N-n-n-no," answered Sam hesitatingly.

"Now, tell me where you put it."

"I told you once. I put it in the muzzle. Where did you think I put it?"

"I did not think. But it is now my opinion that you dropped it overboard."

"I did nothing of the sort," protested Hickey indignantly.

"You were the last man to handle the plug, were you not?"

"Y-e-s."

"Where is it?"

"I—I don't know."

"That will cost you twenty-five, young man. You will no doubt be put on the list for a reprimand, if not worse. That's all I've got to say to you."

Sam stood with both hands thrust in his trousers' pockets, gazing absently off to sea.

"Almost a whole month's pay gone to grass," he muttered. "Shoot the whole business!"

CHAPTER VI

THE RED, WHITE AND BLUE

AN hour later Sam Hickey ran across the fellow Black on the superstructure.

"See here, Blackie."

Black moved on as if he had not heard. A second later Sam had him by the collar.

"You wait a minute. I've got something to say to you."

Black halted because the grip on his collar forced him to do so, but he turned an angry face on the Battleship Boy.

"I'm in a fix, Blackie, and you've got to help me out."

Black grunted.

"You were standing outside the seven-inch port when I came out on deck a while ago, weren't you?"

"Yes."

"You saw me put that tompion in the muzzle of the gun there, didn't you?"

Black shook his head.

"You didn't?"

"Me not see."

"Don't you remember, I was just putting the plug in when I said 'hello' to you, and you

wrinkled up your face as if you had a colic, or
some other kind of pain in your stomach?"
urged Hickey.

Black shook his head again.

"Me see nothing," he declared sullenly.

Sam surveyed him half suspiciously.

"You're a thick-head, that's what you are.
Here I am in a fix, and you won't even try to
help me out. You just wait until you get in
trouble, and see how quickly I will come to your
rescue—not! I'll lose my memory entirely so
far as what you want me to remember is concerned. Go on; I don't want anything more
to do with you," added the red-haired boy,
giving the other a shove.

"What's the trouble, Sam?" demanded Dan
Davis, who was passing along the deck at that
moment.

Sam explained briefly.

"You are sure you put the tompion in the
gun?"

"Sure? Of course I'm sure. I couldn't possibly be mistaken about a thing like that, could
I?"

"I should think not."

"Of course I couldn't."

"Then it must have fallen out and gone overboard. Evidently you did not put it in tightly.
I can't see but that you were negligent, so take

your medicine like a man, Sam. In other words, grin and bear it,'' advised Dan.

"Huh!" grunted Hickey in a tone of disgust. "Twenty-five dollars' worth, eh? All right; I'll bear it, but I'll not grin.''

While this conversation was taking place another was being held in the cabin of the captain, who was in consultation with Mr. Coates, his executive officer.

"I have just received an order by wireless from the admiral to put ashore six signalmen to be used for landing practice up in Gardiner's Bay. They are going ashore this afternoon, when we move up near enough to put them off,'' said the captain. "How many signalmen will that leave us for our work?"

"Let me see,'' mused the executive officer. "It will leave us three men. I presume you wish to send the most expert signalmen to the admiral?"

"By all means.''

"That will leave us very short. We shall be practically without a signal corps. Three of our fellows are merely novices, and can hardly be depended upon.''

"Then I shall have to wire the admiral that we cannot spare the men. I dislike very much to do that, for we should have plenty of men on board who are experts with the wig-wag flags.''

"Yes, that is so. It would be rather humiliating to have to confess our weakness. Is there no other way out of it? Perhaps we could get along without a signal corps for the present."

"Wait a minute. I have an idea," exclaimed the commanding officer, his face lighting with a smile.

"Yes, sir."

"Is not that young seaman, Dan Davis, handy with the flags?"

"Right you are, sir."

"Was he not one of the signalmen who did such fine work when we were laying mines, the time Bill Kester was rescued by this same boy?"

"Yes, sir. Both boys took part in that rescue, if you recall the incident."

"Yes, I remember. That will leave us in fine shape. You will see to it that the signal corps is put ashore this afternoon."

"Yes, sir."

"And, by the way, I think it might be a good idea to have Davis drill in some other men while we are about it. I want to see what we can do. He strikes me as being a most likely lad."

"Both of them are, sir, though Davis is built of a little finer material than his companion. Have I your instructions to order him to go ahead with the instruction?"

"Certainly."

"How many men shall we try out?"

"Oh, say a dozen. From the dozen we shall be able to pick at least six likely ones."

"Shall we assign the men?"

The captain reflected.

"No, let Seaman Davis do that. If he chooses any men we cannot spare you will so advise him. I want to see what sort of material he will choose."

"Very good, sir; I will attend to the matter at once."

Shortly after that Dan received orders to report to the executive officer. The latter explained briefly what was wanted of him.

"For the purpose of the instruction you are clothed with the authority of a petty officer," said Mr. Coates. "Your orders will be obeyed. When you have chosen your men hand me the list, and I will pass upon it."

"Aye, aye, sir."

"You are relieved from further duty for the present."

"Aye, aye, sir."

Dan made a dignified salute, and walked away with his shoulders a little more erect than usual. But the moment he was sure he had gotten out of sight of the officer, he started off on a run to carry the good news to Sam Hickey. Sam was not over enthusiastic. He was still grumbling over the loss of the tompion, which meant also the loss of twenty-five dollars to himself.

Within the hour he had handed in the list of names of the men chosen for signal duty. This list was approved by the executive officer and the captain, and that afternoon Dan assembled his class on the forward deck for their first lesson. Not a man of them had ever before had signal instruction.

In military formation the Battleship Boy marched his class up and out to the forward deck.

"Halt!" he commanded. "Left face! Right dress! Front!"

"Coates, that was pretty well done, eh?" chuckled the captain, who, with his executive officer, was leaning over the bridge railing, watching the proceedings.

"Open order, march!"

The men of the class spread out so that there was plenty of open space in front of each man.

The Battleship Boy gave the men a brief talk on the general subject of signaling, impressing upon them the need of accuracy.

"Do not try to be fast. Speed will come in good time, but make it your ambition both to send and to read messages with absolute accuracy. We will now begin with the code, which is as follows:"

Davis ran through the code, signaling out each letter slowly in order to show the men how the movements were executed.

The wig-wag code, as used in the United States Navy, consists of a series of numbers that represent the letters of the alphabet. They are delivered by a red flag bearing a white square in its center. The code that Dan spelled out is as follows:

A	....	22	O	....	21
B	....	2112	P	....	1212
C	....	121	Q	....	1211
D	....	222	R	....	211
E	....	12	S	....	212
F	....	2221	T	....	2
G	....	2211	U	....	112
H	....	122	V	....	1222
I	....	1	W	....	1121
J	....	1122	X	....	2122
K	....	2121	Y	....	111
L	....	221	Z	....	2222
M	....	1221	End of word........	3
N	....	11	End of sentence.....	33

The flag with which the numbers are made is attached to a staff just long enough to handle easily. Before beginning the message the flag staff is held perpendicularly in front of the operator. Dipping the flag once to the left, at right angles to the body, indicates the figure two.

Dipping it once to the right indicates the figure one. Dipping it forward once, away from the body means the figure three. For instance, if the flag be dipped twice to the left, the operator will have made the signal "twenty-two," meaning A.

"I will now spell the words 'Battleship Boy,'" he said, beginning a slow movement of the wig-wag flag, making the following figures:

"2112, 22, 2, 2, 221, 12, 212, 122, 1, 1212, 3, 2112, 21, 111, 212."

"We will now begin practicing the code in groups of three letters," said the instructor.

For a full hour he put the young jackies through their paces. By the time the bugle blew his class had learned nearly half the signal alphabet.

"If you will practice these movements, using your hands in place of flags, this evening, you will have fixed the numbers and the letters that they represent so firmly in your minds that you will not be likely to forget them. Do it at every opportunity before turning in to-night. I shall expect each of you to be letter-perfect in the morning. Once more, now, call the letters as I make them. I will give you only what you have had this afternoon. Begin with the first man in line."

The Battleship Boys Swung Into the Chorus.

The Battleship Boy made the figures, wig-wagging slowly. Among the men on the forward deck there were only three who were not quick to read the signals. These Dan ordered to step forward. A few minutes proved, to his own satisfaction, that their minds were too sluggish to enable them to make very good signalmen.

"You three men need not report to-morrow," he said.

"That boy is bound to command, Coates," announced the captain with emphasis. "Davis!"

"Aye, aye, sir," answered Dan, turning and saluting.

"You and your friend, Seaman Hickey, turn to and give an exhibition of wig-wagging. It will be instructive, as well as entertaining, to all of us."

Dan's eyes lighted with pleasure.

" 'Red, White and Blue,' " he said, as he passed a flag to Sam. "Follow me giving the next lines."

"Will that save my twenty-five?"

"It may."

"All right, I'll take a chance on it. Go ahead."

Dan stationed himself on one side of the deck, while Sam walked briskly to the opposite side.

"Oh, Columbia, the gem of the ocean,
　　The home of the brave and the free,"

wig-wagged Dan.

"The shrine of each patriot's devotion,
　　A world offers homage to thee,"

continued Sam Hickey, his red flag flashing up
and down forming the letters of the code with
such swiftness that few of the officers were able
to follow.

"Thy mandates make heroes assemble,
　　When Liberty's form stands in view;
Thy banners make tyranny tremble,
　　When borne by the red, white and blue."

The instant Dan's swift strokes with flag had
ended the verse, both the Battleship Boys swung
into the chorus,

"When borne by the red, white and blue,
When borne by the red, white and blue,
Thy banners make tyranny tremble,
When borne by the red, white and blue."

"Thirty-three, thirty-three," finished the lads,
bringing the butts of their flag staffs to the deck
with a click that sounded as one.

A perfect storm of applause from the officers rewarded the splendid performance of the Battleship Boys. The jackies on the deck, though few of them had been able to make out the message, the words of the beautiful anthem, realized that they were watching the work of two masters with the wig-wag flags, so they, too, added their quota to the applause. They did not do so by hand applause. The jackies threw up their hats and set up a loud cheer.

"The most remarkable performance of its kind that I ever saw," announced the captain.

"I never saw anything like it myself," agreed the executive officer. "It's lucky we happened to think of those boys."

"Indeed it is."

"Anything further, sir?" questioned Dan, saluting.

"That will be sufficient. Thank you, my lads."

The boys saluted, then marched from the forecastle, proud and happy, but not forgetting their dignity in their excitement and pleasure.

"Three cheers for the Battleship Boys," shouted one of the bluejackets the instant the officers had left the bridge. "Hurrah for little Dynamite!" That last was Dan's nickname. And the cheers were given with a will.

CHAPTER VII

B Y this time every officer and man on the battleship "Long Island" knew Dan Davis and Sam Hickey by name as well as by sight. But the lads bore their honors well. Neither of the boys sought to take advantage of the favor he had gained. If anything, the boys toiled harder than ever. They worked with the formidable seven-inch gun during all the hours that were allotted to this work.

During the rest hour Dan and his companion would ordinarily be found in the turret, examining the gun and its carriage, quizzing each other to test their knowledge, committing to memory the name and use of every part of these complicated instruments of war.

Late one afternoon, when the men were supposed to be at play on the forward deck, the captain was passing through on his way to his quarters, when he heard voices in the turret and peered in there.

He saw Dan and Sam stripped to their undershirts, working the big gun and going through with their own examination. Dan was trying to explain to his companion the theory and practice of range-finding—learning the distance and location of the enemy. From that they drifted into the question of sighting the big guns, elevation and other technical subjects beyond their years and experience.

The ship's commander smiled proudly. After a few moments of listening, he stepped inside.

"Well, lads, do you never rest?" he questioned, in a kindly tone, for the commanding officer of the "Long Island" was a humane man, one who had the interests of his men at heart to a degree possessed by few commanding officers in the service.

The lads saluted but made no reply, as an answer was not expected to the question.

"Are you studying—I mean in books?"

"Yes, sir," replied Dan.

"Where do you get your books?"

"From the ship's library, sir."

"I am afraid you are in need of some more advanced works than you will find in the crew's library. If you will come to my quarters, this evening after your mess, I will see what I can find for you. I think I have some books that will be of use to you. By the way, I heard you mention electricity once or twice. Do you know anything about that branch?"

"A little, sir, but we are studying that as well," Dan replied.

"From books?"

"Oh, yes, sir. Besides this we are taking a course in electricity with a correspondence school."

The eyes of the commanding officer twinkled.

"You are two very industrious boys. I am afraid not many of our boys are following your example."

"Quite a few of them are, sir."

"May I ask what you are seeking to accomplish?"

Dan glanced up inquiringly.

"I mean as to the future. What do you hope to do with yourself?" asked the captain.

"Naturally, sir, I hope to gain promotion when I have earned it," was Dan's answer.

"Ah, yes; to be sure. You have ambitions to become petty officers. Well, your prospects are good, young men, if you keep on in that way you have been going. You will come below for the books as I suggested, will you not?"

"Yes, sir; thank you, sir."

"As I have said before, whenever you wish advice or assistance, come to me, through your immediate superiors, and you will find me ever ready to aid you."

"Thank you, sir," acknowledged the boys, in chorus. The captain saluted in answer to theirs; then, turning on his heel, left the turret.

"That's what I call a right smart gentleman,"
announced Sam Hickey, with an emphatic nod
of the head.

"The captain is a magnificent man. We are
lucky, old fellow, in being under such a commander. I'd face powder and bullets any day
for him."

"Say, Dan."

"Yes."

"He invited us to call on him, didn't he?"

"Well, yes; something like that, though not
in a social sense. That would be impossible."

Sam pondered.

"Do you know I'd give a month's pay if the
rest of the bunch could see me sitting in one of
those mahogany chairs in the Old Man's quarters, with my feet on his dining room table."

"Sam Hickey, I am ashamed of you. You
ought to be ashamed of yourself, to say a thing
like that! Suppose the commanding officer had
overheard those words, instead of what he did
overhear. What would you have done then?"

"What would I have done? Why, I'd have
slipped out through the gun port, and left you
to square things with him," answered the re-
sourceful Sam.

"You're hopeless," muttered Dan. "And,
another thing, before you talk of giving a
month's pay remember that you have nearly a

month's pay charged against you for the loss of the tompion.''

''That's so. I'm going to ask the captain about that. Maybe, when he hears my side of the case, he will remit the fine. It's a shame to make me pay it.''

''Don't be a baby. Be a man and take your medicine like a man,'' advised Dan, as he pulled on his jacket and prepared to leave the turret.

That evening they reported at the captain's quarters, as they had been directed. While, in this instance, the lads remained standing, their commanding officer talked with them as if they were really his equals; that is, as if there were no social barriers erected between them.

The longer they remained in the service the more the Battleship Boys came to realize that the gulf between officers and men was not nearly so wide as it had been painted. The officer worked by the side of his men in the grime and dirt, and at all times made the comfort of the jackies his personal care. Strict forms, however, had to be lived up to for the sake of discipline.

On the following morning, when the two boys reported to turret number four, where they were stationed, the gun captain lined up his men and looked them over after roll call.

''What we need in this crew, just now, is gun

pointers. Those of you who have tried that work aren't worth the powder to blow you through a ventilator. What we are going to do I'll confess I don't know. Here we are, within four weeks of battle practice, and not one of you could sight a gun so that it would send a ball through a barn if the barn were leaned up against the muzzle. Do any of you who haven't tried think you can sight a seven-inch gun?"

"I used to shoot woodchucks with a shotgun, sir," Sam Hickey informed the gun captain.

The gun crew laughed loudly.

"Bosh!" exploded the gun captain.

"I can shoot, sir," insisted Sam.

"I'd be afraid to have you get near a bag of powder with that fiery head. It's a wonder you don't blow up with spontaneous combustion. You will, one of these times, if you don't look sharp."

A pugnacious look flashed into Sam Hickey's eyes, but he dared not make a retort to the gun captain.

"Davis, do you think you could learn to sight a gun?"

"Yes, sir; I think so."

"You'll get the chance. We will give you a try-out this morning. All hands line up for dotter practice."

"What's dotter practice?" asked Sam.

"Sh-h-h," warned Dan. "Haven't you learned what that is yet?"

"No."

"Dotter practice is target work in miniature. Listen! The gun captain is going to explain it to us."

"Some of you understand the dotter," began the gun captain. "For the benefit of those of you who do not I will explain. The dotter is a little contrivance on the gun, which enables you to shoot at a target and proves your marksmanship. By looking through the finder you will see a little target that moves up and down like a ship at sea. When the crossed wires of your finder are right on the target you pull the trigger. A black spot will appear on the target— a dot, showing where your shot struck if you have hit the target at all. We call it a dotter because it makes a dot where it hits."

"And the dotter makes you dotty," muttered Sam under his breath, yet loudly enough so that the man next to him heard it. The fellow laughed aloud, bringing down a sharp rebuke from the gun captain.

"Hickey, try your hand at the dotter."

Sam climbed up to the little platform on the right side of the gun, winking at his companions as he did so.

"What shall I do now?" he questioned, taking his place.

"Sight through the finder. I'll set the target going."

"Yes, I see it. I'm afraid that thing will make me seasick if I keep on looking at it," declared Hickey, looking up at the instructor.

"Attend to your practice!"

"Bang!"

Sam leaped up into the air. His head came into violent contact with the deck above him.

"Ouch!" yelled the red-headed boy, as he collapsed in a heap on the deck.

Sam had unwittingly pulled the trigger, firing the cap that had been provided to explode the dotter, thus making the miniature target work the more realistic.

"Did something hit me? I—I thought the seven-inch had gone off," stammered the boy, pulling himself to his feet and rubbing his head where it had hit the ceiling.

"Just like a landlubber," growled the gun captain. "You'll make a fine gun pointer, you will."

"I—I didn't know the thing was going off," complained Hickey.

"I suppose, if we were to fire the piece in earnest, you would jump overboard," sneered the

captain. "Get up there, now, and do it right, if
you want to stay in this division."

Sam took his place once more, the gun captain
giving him suggestions and directions as to how
to catch the moving target when it was moving
upward as a ship does in riding a great swell.

"Bang!"

Sam had pulled the trigger, but this time he
had done so intentionally. Instinctively the lad
jumped, grinning sheepishly as he noted the
smiles on the faces of his companions of the
gun crew.

"Well, what is your score?"

"Score?"

"Yes. Did you hit the target?"

"I don't know."

"Look at the target."

"I see a fly speck over by the edge of the
target," spoke up Sam.

"That is where your shot struck. Had you
been shooting at a battleship you might have
raked her stern, but I reckon you would not have
done her very great damage. However, it was
not a half-bad shot for a landlubber. Number
three, take your place."

The man indicated made an even worse shot
than had Hickey, though he had been practising
with the dotter for three weeks.

"You never will do at this work," decided

the gun captain. "About all you will be good for will be to clean bright work and pass along ammunition. Davis, let's see what you can do."

Dan was all expectation. He could hardly wait for his turn at the gun.

"You understand how to work it?"

"I think so."

"Take your time. Make sure of your mark, then let go quickly. You will find in actual target work, or in shooting at an enemy, that a fraction of a second's delay will ordinarily roll the target out of your range. Better to shoot a second too soon than a second too late."

Dan was peering through the sights, his eye fixed on the pin-head opening. One hand crept slowly to the trigger. It rested there for a few seconds without a tremor. His nerves were steady and true.

"Bang!"

"What luck?"

"Squarely in the center. That's what I should call a bull's eye," announced Dan Davis triumphantly. "Am I right, sir?"

"Yes; you hit the mark all right. It may have been a chance shot."

"I think not, sir. I will see if I can do it again."

Dan applied his eye to the finder. An instant's hesitation, then there followed the sharp report of the dotter.

"Once more in the center, sir. Shall I fire again?"

"No. You've sunk the ship, young man. You have put the enemy out of business. You are not only going to make a splendid gunner, but you are far above the average already."

Ere Dan could express his thanks the bugle blew, piping gun crews down to other duties.

CHAPTER VIII

THE "Long Island" was still lying inside the breakwater when the lads were piped to their gun station the following morning.

"Seaman Dan Davis and Sam Hickey will hereafter act as gun pointers in number four turret," said the gun captain. "You will get your rating badges at the canteen, meaning the ship's storeroom. See that you have them before the afternoon practice at four bells."

The Battleship Boys looked at each other triumphantly, and Sam winked wisely at his companion. How the lads did go through their work that day, performing each duty with a snap that drew nods of approval from the gun captain and wondering looks from their companions.

After the noon meal they hastened to the canteen, where they procured the rating badges. This was a square of blue cloth on which was a white circle with two fine lines drawn across the circle at right angles to each other, representing the crossed sights such as one finds in a telescope rifle.

The boys lost no time in sewing them on
their sleeves, after which they paraded the forward deck, doing their best to look uncon-
cerned. Their efforts in this direction were
failures.

"Hello, Dynamite! I see you've got your
hash marks," greeted a companion.

"Oh, you mean this," answered Dan, with
glowing face, as he held up his arm.

"I've got one, too, even if I couldn't hit the
side of a barn," spoke up the red-headed
Hickey. "I told the captain of number four
how I had plugged woodchucks back home,
though, and I guess that convinced him that
I could shoot big guns."

"Say, Hickey, speaking of hash marks, have
you got any on you yet?"

"I'm just telling you I have one here. I'm
a gun pointer. If you don't believe it, come
over to the turret and I'll point one at you.
It'll make you jump when the pop-gun goes
off, I'll bet."

"No, no; I don't mean that kind of a hash
mark," laughed his companion."

"What kind, then?"

"Tattoo marks. We call them hash marks."

"I get tattooed—is that what you mean?"

"Of course; every sailor—every real sailor—
has that done."

"What for?"

"Just to be the real thing; that's all."

"I don't know. I hadn't thought of it."

"I'll take you over to Needle Johnson, if you want to have it done."

"Well, I don't know," reflected Sam. "Does it hurt?"

"Of course it doesn't. You will not even feel it. Doesn't hurt half as much as the sting of a Jersey mosquito."

"I'll go and talk with What's-his-name——"

"Needle Johnson."

"Yes. Where's Dan?"

"I think he has gone below. You come along, and he'll be surprised and envious when he finds you have had the job done," continued the boy's shipmate with a wink at some of the others standing by.

Sam somewhat reluctantly followed the jackie below, where, after some searching about, they finally located Needle Johnson. Needle was an old-time sea dog, wearing a heavy crop of whiskers and with a voice that would have done credit to a boatswain's mate.

"Here's a lad who hasn't had a hash mark put on his skin, and he's been on board for three months."

Needle gazed at the red-headed boy pityingly.

"You don't mean it?"

"Yes. I told him he wouldn't be a real sailor until he had some paint stuck under his hide."

"That's the sure thing, my lad, and I'm the salt that can give you the purtiest hashings you ever set eyes on. Where did you reckon you wanted the marks put?"

"I hadn't reckoned anything about it. I guess I don't want any of those hash marks, as you call them," Sam returned.

"What? Not want them? Of course you do."

Sam reflected a moment, then gave a reluctant consent.

"What kind of a tattoo would you suggest?"

"A pig's foot, by all means, matey. That's the latest and most fashionable decoration that a gentleman can wear. How'll you have it?"

"I'll take mine pickled, if it's all the same to you," answered Sam soberly.

The jackies roared.

"What do you take me for—a sea-cook?" growled Johnson. "Take off your right shoe if you want to do business with me."

"What for?"

"For the hash. You wouldn't have a pig's foot anywhere else, would you?"

"I—I don't know."

"That's the only place to put it, and it will bring you luck."

In the meantime Needle Johnson had gotten out his case of needles and his coloring matter.

"You are sure it won't hurt?" asked Sam.

"You won't feel a thing. Now, hold perfectly still. If you jerked, or anything, I might make a pig's tail instead of a pig's foot. That would be tough, wouldn't it, matey?"

"It might be tough for you. Ou-u-u-uch!"

Sam Hickey's foot came up with such suddenness that Needle was unable to dodge it. The foot caught Needle fairly on the nose, bowling him over to the deck, while all hands were shrieking with delight over his discomfiture.

"What—what do you mean, you—you lubber?" demanded Needle angrily, rubbing the injured member, then shaking a fist under the red-headed boy's nose.

"You—you said it wouldn't hurt."

"Hurt nothing!"

"I should say it did hurt. What are you trying to do—drill a hole all the way through my foot? I don't want any hash marks. I'll get along with just my natural skin, whether I have any luck or not. Give me that shoe."

"Say, fellows," spoke up a jackie. "I reckon Red-head had better have a pig's foot, eh?"

"You bet he had," chorused the others.

"And he won't do it of his own free will."

"So he says."

"Then it seems to be our solemn duty to take the job into our own hands, does it not, mates?"

"It is."

"All right, then. Seaman Hickey, do we get it straight that you defy the rules of our profession by refusing to wear the badge of that profession?"

"Call it what you want to. I'm not going to have any heathen rites performed over me, or my skin pricked full of holes."

"Then, shipmate, you'll have to take your medicine. Jump on him, boys!"

Black and White, the two Hawaiians who had been standing by grinning, made a concerted rush for Hickey. He wheeled just as they threw themselves upon him. But the Pacific Islanders were reckoning without the cost.

"So that's the game, is it?" gritted Sam.

Grabbing Black by the collar and one leg, he pitched the fellow half way across the deck, standing the Hawaiian on his head. White followed. He, too, was sailing through the air before Black struck. Both landed on the same spot, and instantly were fighting each other in their efforts to get clear.

But the admiring jackies had no time to spare.

They would have liked nothing better than to have let that affair go on to a finish. Instead, the whole crowd, fifteen or twenty of them, fell upon the red-haired boy, hand and foot. Sam went down in a heap. He was not angry, but he was giving these fellows all they wanted in their attempts to hold him down.

"Grab the foot!" shouted one.

The jackie did so, but was promptly knocked over by a kick on the nose, causing that member to bleed freely.

This time two sailors grasped the Battleship Boy's naked foot and straightened it out.

"Get your tools out, Needle. Here's your foot."

Despite their efforts, the foot was working back and forth so fast that Johnson was unable to do anything with it.

"Pass a rope around it. That's the way we used to rope cattle out west. That's the idea."

A line was passed about Hickey's ankle and made fast to a stanchion.

"All right, Needle, drive the color in deep, so it won't wash out."

"Give him two pig's feet," suggested another. "He'll have better luck if you do."

"I'll trim the whole bunch of you for this," growled a voice from the bottom of the pile.

The jackies laughed loudly.

"Me fix him, me fix him," snarled Black, at
that instant jumping into the pile, his face con-
torted with rage.

"You get out and mind your own business,"
advised one of the men. "You got yours; now
run along and be good. Take your white friend
along with you, while you are about it, or we'll
paint both of you."

While this conversation was going on Johnson was plying his needle industriously, and
under his hand Sam Hickey's foot was under-
going a great change. Little by little the outline of a pig's foot was appearing. The pig's
foot was done in red, while the toe nails of
the foot were in blue.

"There; you can let the broncho up now,"
announced Johnson, after putting the final
touches to his artistic achievement.

The sailors piled off, while one of their number released the rope that held the foot. Sam
struggled to a sitting posture, much the worse
for wear, his hair standing up, his clothes soiled
and disordered. But it was the foot that attracted his attention. He surveyed it dubiously,
then his eyes wandered about the circle of
laughing faces.

Sam grinned a sheepish grin.

"Fellows, you've insulted an officer and a
gentleman, and I've got to get even with you

—no; I'll have you before the mast, every one of you, so——"

All hands began grunting in imitation of a herd of pigs.

"I see I am not the only pig in the sty, after all," announced Seaman Hickey cuttingly, as he calmly began pulling on his shoe over the sore foot.

CHAPTER IX

"COLORS! Fall in for colors!" shouted petty officers in different parts of the ship as the bugle blew its warning notes.

Sam Hickey limped into place with the gun squad, and awaited the order to march.

"Colors," means the formalities that are observed at sunset on shipboard, consisting of impressive ceremonies when the Stars and Strips are lowered from the after flagstaff. The ceremony of colors, however, is never observed when the ship is under motion, but only when the vessel is at anchor.

Just before the moment when the sun was to set, the different divisions, in charge of midshipmen and ensigns, were marched to the quarterdeck with measured step; then, facing toward amidships, they banked themselves on each side of the deck. Behind the jackies, next to the starboard and port rails, were the marines, carrying their rifles.

Grouped aft on the starboard side was the band, its members resplendent in white and gold uniforms.

Between these lines of color stood the captain and his executive officer, facing the Flag that was lazily fluttering in the soft evening breeze.

All was silence, the only sound being the water lapping the steel sides of the battleship.

"Attention!"

The bugle blew a few short notes. The Flag began creeping slowly down the after flagstaff, with every eye fixed on the ensign as it fluttered toward the deck.

Instantly upon the Flag's reaching the deck, the band broke forth into "The Star Spangled Banner." The hearts of the Battleship Boys swelled with patriotism, and the strains of the national anthem seemed to bring a deeper shade to the rows of tanned, manly faces lined up in solid ranks on the quarter-deck of the battleship "Long Island."

"Attention! First division, right face! Forward march!"

The command was repeated for the other divisions. Snare drums rolled, the band changed to a livelier tune, to which each division marched off in steady lines, one division following the other. Soon all had disappeared, save a group of officers who remained chatting on the quarter-deck. These, too, soon turned and went below for the evening mess.

The day's work was done for all except those who were to go on watch duty for a two-hour trick.

Mess finished, Sam went out to the forward deck to growl at the jackies who had been responsible for the pig's foot on his own right foot. The pig's foot hurt him, and the lad limped painfully.

While Sam was forward Dan got out his ditty box, to which, by this time, he had become as much attached as were the other sailors to theirs. From the box he drew a recent letter from his mother, which the Battleship Boy, sitting on the steel deck under a wall lamp in a corridor, read over several times. It seemed a long time to Dan since he had left her at Piedmont, and had gone on to New York to enlist in the service of his country.

"I think I must know this letter by heart," mused Dan, folding the letter and tenderly laying it away in the precious ditty box. Then, fixing up his fountain pen, he began writing industriously, using his elevated knees for a desk, on which he had laid his writing pad.

"I have written in more comfortable places than this, but I never had more to say than I have this time," he said.

Mails were not very regular on shipboard,

and sometimes it was a matter of weeks before a single mail was put over the side.

Dan was still writing, an hour later, when Sam came along looking for him.

"Oh, here you are, eh?"

"Yes."

"Writing a book?"

"No, I'm writing to mother. Is there any word you would like to send to the folks at Piedmont?"

"You might say hello to Mrs. Davis for me. If they'd let a fellow change his mind in this business, you'd see me back there to-morrow. What are you writing to her?"

Dan smiled quizzically.

"If it were anyone else who asked me that question I might tell him it was none of his business."

"But you don't dare tell me that, hey?"

"Maybe, Sam," answered Dan with a good-natured laugh.

"All right; what you are telling her?"

"Want to know very much?"

"I shouldn't have asked you if I didn't."

"Very well; I'll tell you. You know I have something more than two hundred dollars laid up with the paymaster——"

"Yes; aren't you afraid the Jack-o'-the-Dust will run away with it?"

"Hardly. Even if he does, the Government would make the amount good."

"What you going to do with the money?"

"I was about to tell you. That is what I am writing to mother about. I am sending the money to her."

"All of it?" interrupted Sam.

"Yes, of course. Why not?"

"You're a good sport, you are."

"I am telling her to go buy a lot out on the Perkins road. That amount will just about purchase one. Then, as fast as I earn more money, I tell her, I will send it to her, and by next summer she will have enough to go on and build a house. Mother will have a home of her own then, and I'll feel much better when she has."

"How much does a house cost in that neck-o'-the-woods?"

"Well, I should say that eight hundred dollars will put up a very fair place. At least, it will satisfy us. Why do you ask?"

"I was thinking. Say, did you hear about my pig's foot?"

"Your pig's foot?"

"Yes."

"I don't know what you mean."

"I've got one on my right foot."

"I haven't the least idea what you are talking about."

"You would have, if you'd got a pig's foot. It's a lot different from a rabbit's foot, and don't you make any mistake about that."

"Somebody gave you a pig's foot, for luck, eh? I never heard they were lucky."

"Oh, yes; they gave it to me, all right. Here, look at this."

Sam pulled off a shoe and stocking, exhibiting his freshly tattooed foot.

"Well, what do you think of that?" marveled Dan.

"Not much," growled Sam.

"Who did it?"

"Old Pin Head—No, I mean old Needle Johnson."

"Why did you let him do that, Sam?"

"Let him? I didn't. The whole forecastle sat on me, and tied my foot up to a stanchion, while the head butcher performed the operation. I can hardly walk. But I forgot to tell you. Those black-faced fellows from the other side of the world sailed into me as if they wanted to eat me up. I don't like that pair a little bit, Dan."

"Imagination, Sam. Just because they are a little darker than we are, you do not like them. That is foolish."

"That's just the trouble. If it was only skin deep I wouldn't give a rap. The trouble with those fellows is that the black goes all the way through. I'll bet they are black clear to the bones. If Pills ever has to cut either of them open for anything I'm going to take a peek.''

"I am surprised at you, Sam,'' chided Davis.

"You needn't be. You'll find, one of these days, that I am right. But how about that house and lot?"

"If you keep on talking to me, hammocks will be piped up before I finish my letter.''

"Go on with your writing. I'm mum.'' Sam sat down and was soon lost in deep thought.

"There,'' announced Dan finally. "I guess that's all I can write to-night. I've done eight pages. That's pretty good for a sailor.''

"I never wrote as much as that in all my life —that is, I never wrote as much as that in letters. Say, Dan.''

"Yes.''

"Do you mind if I say a few words to Mother Davis at the end of your letter?''

"Of course, you may. Mother will be delighted.''

"All right. You go outside and take a walk for your health. I can't write with anybody looking at me. It makes me nervous.''

"Too bad about your sensitive nerves,'' retorted the other with a laugh. "All right; I'll

go out. Do not be long, for it is nearly hammock time.''

Leaving Sam grumbling about having to go to
bed at nine o'clock, Dan strolled out on the deck.

''Dear Mother Davis,'' began Sam, ''I want
to tell you that your Dan isn't the only jackie
who has money. I've got two hundred dollars,
too. But I haven't any mother. The two hundred isn't any good to me. I've been thinking
of giving it to the government some of these
times, for they could use it where it would do
some good. I've got a new idea, now. I'm going to send the two hundred to you, along with
Dan's. You start that house right away, and, by
the time all the money is used up, Dan and I will
have some more for you. We're getting too rich.
If Dan kicks about it, you know how to stop him.
P. S. I'm a real sailor, now. I've got a rating
and a pig's foot. The rating made me glad,
but the pig's foot hurt worse than having a
tooth pulled. Lovingly, Sam.''

CHAPTER X

LEAVING Sam in the throes of composition, Dan walked out on deck. A few moments later he uttered a sharp exclamation and clapped a hand to his left ear, through which he felt a sudden, sharp pain. As he brought the hand away, the fingers felt wet.

Dan stepped up under a port light that opened out to the deck, and, holding up the fingers, peered at them.

"Blood, eh! Well, that's funny. Something must have hit me."

He glanced about him. He was almost alone; there were not a half dozen sailors on deck, and these lay stretched out, sleeping soundly in the cool evening air.

"That is strange," wondered the lad, trying to stanch the flow of blood with his handkerchief. He had been about to turn back and rejoin Sam when the incident occurred.

Dan paused to think over just what had happened.

"Oh, I remember, now. I heard something strike the deck. That must have been after it hit me. I'll see if I can find out what it was."

Stepping carefully along over the deck, feeling with his toes, the boy almost tripped over some object which he knew did not belong there.

With an exclamation Dan stooped over. His hand came in contact with a piece of cold steel. The instant his fingers touched it he knew what he had found.

"A marline spike," breathed Dan. "No wonder it hurt."

The missile that had hit him is used for twisting the strands of rope apart. It is of steel, about eight inches long, and tapers to a needle point. It makes a most dangerous weapon.

Dan carried this to the light, examining it carefully. Its point was still moist where it had caught him.

"Somebody must have tried to kill me," he muttered. "An inch further, and I certainly should have been a dead one. Who could have done such a dastardly thing? I can't understand it at all."

The lad hurried back to where he had left his companion. Sam started to speak, but he saw something in the face of Dan Davis that suddenly checked his levity.

"Why, what's the matter?" he cried.

"Nothing, except that some one tried to kill me just now."

"Tried to kill you?"

"Yes; look here."

Dan removed the handkerchief, and Sam, with gentle fingers, made a careful examination of the wound.

"Punched a hole right through the lobe of your ear. Who did that?" he demanded in a low, tense voice.

"I wish I knew."

"How did they do it? It looks as if you had been shot."

"They did it with this, Sam," answered Dan, exhibiting the marline spike.

Sam uttered a low growl, as he took the pointed spike, holding it in his hand reflectively.

"You must have that dressed, right away. Come along. We'll go to see Pills. There is time, if we hurry."

"Yes; I guess it had better be attended to. I shall have such a big ear to-morrow that they will not have me on deck."

"Worse cauliflower ear than you gave Bill Kester," laughed Sam. "We'll look into this business in the morning. We shan't have time to-night, I'm sorry to say."

On their way to the sick bay, where they were hurrying to have the wound dressed, the boys were obliged to pass the quarters of the master-at-arms, the minor official who is responsible for the behavior of all hands on shipboard.

Ere Dan could protest, Sam had rapped on the door casing, and an instant later was dragging his companion in through the curtained doorway.

"Now what do you think of that, sir?" exclaimed the red-headed boy.

"Seaman Davis got hurt, eh?" questioned the petty officer, noting the blood on Dan's cheek.

"Yes, sir. I am on my way to see the surgeon. If I have to be a few moments late in reporting for hammocks, will you excuse me?"

"Certainly. I will give you a half hour's leeway. How did you get that wound?"

"Somebody handed him a marline spike, sir," interrupted Hickey.

"A marline spike?"

"Yes, they did."

The master-at-arms turned inquiringly on Dan.

"Is this true?"

Dad nodded half reluctantly.

"Tell me how it occurred."

The boy did so briefly.

"You have no idea who threw the spike?"

"Not the slightest, sir."

"Where were you, Hickey?"

"Below, writing a letter. I knew nothing about it, until my chum came below and I saw the blood on his face."

"Have you any enemies on board?"

"Not that I know of, sir."

"Was anyone except yourself on deck at the time?"

"Yes; a few of the men were asleep further forward. I saw no one moving about."

"Come with me."

The master-at-arms conducted Dan to the surgeon, where a quick examination was made of the wound, after which the surgeon dressed it and put in several stitches. Dan did not even wince, though the pain was severe. Sam's face was pale, and the perspiration stood out on his forehead as he watched the stitching of the ragged ear-lobe.

"Anybody would think you were being operated upon by the looks of you," laughed Dan.

"I feel as if I were," answered Sam rather weakly.

The wound attended to, the petty officer directed the boys to follow him, which they did, going directly to the forward deck.

"Show me where and how you were standing at the time of the accident, Davis."

Dan took the place, as nearly as he could, where he had been standing when the marline spike struck him.

"Which way were you facing?"

"Forward, sir."

"The spike was thrown from behind you then?"

"Yes, sir, it must have been."

"Here is where it hit the deck, sir," called Sam.

"Do you recall how it appeared when you took hold of it?"

"I think the head of the spike was leaning aft. I should say it had about a forty-degree lean."

The master-at-arms nodded.

"It is quite clear that the spike was thrown at you from the superstructure. By the way, where's the spike?"

"I have it," said Sam, extending the spike to the petty officer.

"I will take care of this. Say nothing about what has occurred, but keep your eyes open. If you have reason to suspect any one, let me know at once. I can hardly believe that we have a man on board the 'Long Island' desperate enough to attempt a crime like this. If ever there was an attempted murder this is one. Go to your quarters now."

In the excitement following the attempt on his life, Dan had forgotten all about the letter he had written to his mother. It did not occur to him until the boys were at gun practice with the seven-inch piece the following morning. He turned to Sam at the first opportunity.

"What did you do with my letter?" he demanded.

"I put it in my ditty box last night. I was too excited to remember that it belonged to you. I'll give it to you when we are piped down for mess."

"All right; I want to add something to it."

"Say, Dynamite," said a companion, "where did you get the game ear?"

"It was hurt," answered Dan evasively.

"It looks as if a bulldog had been chewing at it. You never did that of your own accord, did you?"

"That is a foolish question. It isn't likely that I would tear half my ear off, just for the fun of the thing, is it?"

Further conversation was interrupted by an order from the gun captain to resume dotter practice. For the next hour the attention of the boys was wholly taken up by this fascinating work.

After mess Dan asked for his letter. Sam got out his ditty box and handed the letter back rather sheepishly; after which he busied himself with pawing over the articles in his box.

"Am I to read what you have written?" questioned Dan with a smile.

"You may read it, if you want to," answered

Sam, growing very red. "I didn't figure on
your doing so, though."

"Well, you insisted on knowing what I had
written to mother, so I guess you will have to
take the same medicine," retorted Dan with a
laugh, as he opened the sheet on which his companion had written his message to Mrs. Davis.

Dan's face sobered as he read, but he made
no comment until he had gone through the letter. He glanced up with swimming eyes. Sam
was not looking at him. The red-headed boy was
deeply absorbed in his ditty box at that moment.

"Sam Hickey, look at me," commanded Dan.

"I'm looking at you."

"Do you mean that you want to give your
two hundred dollars to mother?"

"Yes, that's what I mean," answered Sam,
defiantly. "I haven't any mother. Why
shouldn't I give your mother my money? I
haven't any use for it, except what I need for
clothes, and I reckon I've got clothes enough to
last me to the end of the cruise. By that time
I'll have another wad. Don't you say a word.
I've made up my mind. Maybe your mother
would fix up a place in the garret where I could
sleep when I go back home again."

"In the garret? Well, I should think not.
The best bedroom in the house will be none too
good for you, Sam Hickey, and that without

your contributing to the house fund either. I can't have it. I——"

"Then I'll sling my hammock in the back yard and roost with the hens. That will be as good as some places I have had to sleep in since I joined the Navy."

"I can't have it, Sam," answered Dan firmly. "No, I cannot accept your gift. Remember, old fellow," added Dan, grasping his companion by the hand, "you owe so much to yourself that you have no business to be generous."

"There's the captain's orderly," interrupted Sam. "I guess he is looking for us. I hope nothing is wrong."

"Are you Seaman Davis?" asked the orderly, who on this occasion was one of the marines.

"Yes."

"The captain wishes to see you in his office before you are piped up to work again."

"I will be there at once. Sam, we'll talk this matter over later. But, remember, I shall not listen to your doing what you have planned, but I'll send your letter to mother so she may know what a great big-hearted fellow you are. I must go now."

Sam had his way, however, and the money went with the letter.

CHAPTER XI

D AN hurried aft, without delay, for a summons from the captain meant that no unnecessary delay would be tolerated. Dan reported and the orderly announced him. The lad entered the captain's office, which was also used as a dining room and stood waiting for his superior to speak.

Dan's ear was done up in adhesive plaster, and a bandage had been wound under his chin and up over his head, giving him the appearance of being much worse off than he really was.

"Davis, I hear you have had an accident?"

"Yes, sir; a slight one, sir. It is of no great consequence, sir."

"I understand differently. I should say that it is of greater consequence than you imagine. The master-at-arms is quite sure that an attempt has been made to do you serious injury, if not worse."

"Perhaps it was not so bad as that, sir. It was a pretty close call, just the same. I am sorry to have been the cause of so much disturbance on board, sir."

"I am sorry, too, but not for that reason. I

am sorry, deeply grieved that there is a man
on board the 'Long Island' base enough to commit, or attempt to commit, such a crime. It is
quite evident that you had a very narrow escape.
I trust you are not suffering greatly from the
wound?''

''Very little, sir.''

''I am glad of that.''

''Thank you, sir.''

''In view of the fact that you are the person
most directly interested, outside of myself, I
have sent for you to direct you to devote every
effort toward learning who your assailant was.
It is of vital importance that we locate the man
and send him up for general court-martial. Of
course, he will be severely punished and then
dismissed from the service. You have no sus-
picions?''

''None at all, sir.''

''Have you had any difficulty with any of the
men?''

''Not that I can recall at the present moment,
sir. I would not intentionally give any man
cause for such enmity.''

''I am sure of that, lad. Have you watched
the men who might possibly have been impli-
cated in this?''

''I have not had an opportunity, sir. And,
besides, I should not know whom to watch. I

am wholly at a loss to account for the attempt."

"I understand. But keep your eyes open. You will be the best person to find the man. You will feel instinctively that you have the right man, before any of the rest of us could have a suspicion. Have your friend do a little investigating also. I have an idea that he is a very shrewd boy. If either of you need any leisure time in which to make your investigations, then inform the master-at-arms, and say that I told you to do so. I trust to your good sense to carry on this investigation in a discreet manner."

"I think you may trust us, sir. I am as anxious as anyone to find the man who did this to me," touching his ear gingerly.

"How are you getting along with your work on the seven-inch?"

"Fairly, sir. I find there is a great deal to learn. May I ask your advice, sir?"

"Go on, lad. I am listening."

"I have been thinking that I should like to take a course in one of the seaman-gunner classes at the Torpedo Station in Newport. Will you tell me, sir, what to do to enter such a class?"

"Certainly. Your ambition is a laudable one. However, you have not been in the service long enough for that as yet. I should advise you to continue your duties on shipboard for a year longer. Then you will be well fitted for the gunner class. Your marks on shipboard must average seventy-five per cent. That will entitle you to admission. The course is six months. In it you will learn the assembling of guns and everything to do with the practical part of ordnance. I can give you some further books along this line, if you wish."

"I do, indeed, sir. I find I have considerable leisure time in which to study. I am working for promotion."

"With your ability, my lad, you will get promotion eventually without going to the school. But it will be an excellent idea for you to go. There you will learn theory as well as practice. After you have served a year, then, it might not be a bad idea to take the eight months' course at the Torpedo Station, where you will learn all about torpedoes and mines. If you hope to rise in the service you will have to know all this, and more. Do you know anything of navigation?"

"Yes, sir; I am studying that now."

"Excellent. Who is teaching you?"

"I am teaching myself."

"I would suggest that you have one of the quartermasters help you. He will do so gladly, and you will possibly avoid falling into errors that you will find troublesome later in your course.''

''Yes, sir.''

''That will be all. The bugle is piping gun crews up, so you had better go to your station. Ord'ly!''

The orderly stepped in and saluted.

''Tell the chief quartermaster that I wish to see him when he is at leisure.''

''Yes, sir.''

Dan hastened to his station, more proud than ever. He could hardly wait until the crew was piped down again to tell Hickey of the encouragement he had received from the commanding officer. Dan determined that Sam should go with him when the time came to go to the gunners' class at Newport, and, with that in view, he had a long talk with his chum that afternoon, urging him to study and work hard that he might be far enough advanced to take the course.

At quarters that night Dan Davis's name was called among those who were to go on watch. He was to take the anchor watch, which would place him on the quarter-deck from eight until twelve o'clock. Both lads had had other watches, but this was the first time either had been on anchor watch, the watch that is always set when the vessel is in port or at anchor.

The Battleship Boy was pleased. Only those

men in whom their superiors had confidence, were ever chosen for these duties, for no little responsibility rests on the watch, especially at night.

The lad's superior on this watch was a midshipman named Carter, a clean-cut, bright young officer who had on several occasions had opportunity to speak to Dan complimenting him on certain well-performed duties.

"Davis, are you on watch to-night?" he asked as Dan approached, saluting.

"Yes, sir."

"How is your wound?"

"Improving, sir, thank you."

"Seeing you are on anchor watch with me, I will let you take charge of the extra-duty squad."

This squad is obliged to remain on duty after the regular hours of work because of some trifling offences. In such cases it is customary to give the squad some light work to do. Now and then the men would be obliged to stand at attention with their rifles for half an hour at a time. Different officers employ different methods with their extra-duty squads.

"Aye, aye, sir," answered Dan, his heart giving a jump, for this was to be his first real command. To all intents he was an officer. He was to command this unhappy squad of shipmates and assist in their punishment. When this thought came to him the boy did not feel half so elated as he had been a moment before.

"What do you wish me to do with them, sir?"

"I will leave that to you. They are not doing anything just now. Perhaps you had better march them about the deck for a time. However, do as you think best."

Dan walked over to where the six delinquents were standing ruefully, with guns over their shoulders.

"Men, I am to have charge of you during this watch. How long are you to be on duty?"

"Two hours, sir."

"You are to be released at ten o'clock, then?"

"Yes, sir."

"Very good. We will now have a few moments in the manual of arms. "Attention! Present arms! Carry arms! Port arms! Right face! Carry arms! Forward march!

The midshipman smiled as the measured tramp of feet attracted his attention, the extra-duty squad in single file marching steadily toward the stern of the vessel.

"Column right, march! Column right, march! Halt!"

The men halted. They were now facing the superstructure.

"Right face!"

"Men, I am going to form you into a guard. Count off."

"One, two, three, four, five, six," counted the men.

"Numbers one and two will take the forward end of the deck, three and four the port and starboard sides respectively, with numbers five and six at the stern. Each set will march back and forth from opposite ends of their stations, patroling their beats. You will carry yourselves like soldiers. Remember, you are on guard duty. You are responsible for this part of the ship. Let no person pass unless he is halted, and then gives the countersign."

"What is the countersign, sir?"

Dan reflected. He had not thought of that. It would not do to let them see that he was at a loss to answer the question.

"I think, men," said Dan, with a smile, "that a pretty good countersign for you will be 'Never again.' Yes, that is the countersign. To your posts, forward march!"

Six faces, reflecting as many grins of appreciation, marched to their posts, which they began patroling, marching back and forth in opposite directions.

The midshipman, officer of the deck, halted

in his leisurely pacing up and down the deck, glancing at the sentries with a puzzled look.

"Now what is that boy Davis up to, I should like to know?" he wondered. "Ah, I see. He has turned out a guard. Not a half-bad idea, at that. He will do. He ought to be an officer, with such resourcefulness as he shows on every occasion."

The officer of the deck resumed his walk, forgetting all about the formation for which Dan was responsible. But it was brought to his notice in a most forcible manner half an hour later.

The night was moonless, and heavy clouds had settled down, enshrouding the ship in a gloom that was broken here and there by the faint rays from a port hole.

Shortly after nine o'clock the captain came up from below for a look at the weather and a breath of fresh air before turning in. He paused at the top of the hatchway, glanced about the deck, then started pacing up and down as was the midshipman doing on the opposite side.

"Halt!" ordered a voice sternly.

The captain glanced up in surprise. He found himself facing a Krag rifle.

"What—what——"

"Who goes there?"

"A friend," he answered instinctively.

"Advance, friend, and give the countersign."

Something of the truth began to dawn upon the quick mind of the commanding officer.

"I do not know the countersign, my man. But I am the commander of this ship."

"Officer of the deck, sir," called the sentry.

The officer of the deck hastened to the spot.

"Sir, stranger without the countersign."

"Man, what do you mean? This is the captain of this ship whom you have halted. What do you mean?"

"Orders, sir, to let no one pass unless he has the countersign."

"Who is responsible for this?" demanded the captain in a half amused tone.

"I let young Davis take charge of the extra-duty squad, and he formed the men into a guard. They had been patroling the deck for the last hour. I did not interfere, not having any idea the affair would be carried this far, sir. I'm sorry, sir. Man, lower your gun."

"Wait, wait!" exclaimed the captain, raising a restraining hand. "This man has his orders. He is quite right. It is a most excellent idea. Fine training for these young men. What is the countersign, Carter?"

"I—I don't know, sir."

"What, you the officer of the deck and not

know the countersign? I am surprised, sir. Where is Seaman Davis?''

"He was here a moment ago."

Dan at that moment was peering from behind the twelve-inch-gun turret, fairly aghast at the situation in which his efforts to do something original had involved them.

"Davis!" called the officer of the deck, in a sharp voice.

"This is where I get it!" muttered the boy. "Aye, aye, sir," he answered promptly, stepping from behind the turret and hastening toward the group.

"What does this farce mean, sir?" demanded the midshipman.

"I will attend to this, Mr. Carter. Davis, these are your men, are they not?"

"Ye—yes, sir."

"You ordered them to let no one pass unless he had the countersign?"

"Yes, sir."

"My man, you did quite right," announced the captain, addressing the sentry. "Davis, will you be good enough to give me the countersign?"

" 'Never again,' " whispered Dan in the ear of his commanding officer.

"What's that? I asked you for the countersign."

"The countersign is 'never again.' "

For a moment the captain stared, then he roared with laughter.

" 'Never again,' my man," he said, whereat the sentry instantly lowered his rifle.

"Well, if that doesn't beat anything I ever heard!" chuckled the captain, grasping Dan by the arm and leading him over to the starboard side of the deck.

CHAPTER XII

"DAVIS, that was a stroke of genius on your part."

"I—I beg your pardon, sir. I did not think how far my thoughtlessness might carry us. I am very sorry, sir."

"You need not be, my lad. If some of our men had as much good sense as you have, there would be fewer extra-duty squads on the quarter-deck. The effect on those men will be most excellent. Besides learning to obey orders, they will carry the memory of that countersign with them for many a day, and unless they are beyond hope of reform, you will not see them on an extra-duty tour again for a long time. I commend you, Davis. You may dismiss the squad now. They need no further lessons for to-night."

"Captain's orders, sir, to dismiss the squad," announced Dan, stepping up before the officer of the deck and saluting.

"Very well. Get my raincoat if you will, then, for I think it is going to rain before the end of the watch."

Dan saluted and hurried away below to fetch

the officer's rain clothes. A light sprinkle set in that soon covered everything, making the decks slippery; it became hard to keep one's footing. Both the officer of the deck and the anchor watch pulled their rubber coats more closely about them, and, with lowered heads to protect their faces from the drizzle, began walking back and forth.

Eleven o'clock, six bells, rang out; then silence settled over the ship again. Cautiously a head was thrust above the hatch of the upper deck. No one was in sight, save the dark figures of the midshipman and the anchor watch, far aft on the quarter-deck.

The head lengthened out into a dark figure, which was drawn up through the hatch opening. Without a sound the man slunk across the deck. He appeared to be perfectly familiar with his way, but crouched low, probably so that his moving figure might not catch the watchful eyes of the officer of the deck, or of the anchor watch far below him.

About this time Dan Davis climbed the ladder to the superstructure, took a long, sweeping observation of the upper deck, then descended to the quarter-deck again.

"I thought I heard something up there," he muttered. "It must have been a chain shifting with the roll of the ship."

In the meantime the figure had flattened itself on the deck.   When sure that the anchor
watch had gone aft, the man rose and crept
silently toward the side of the ship.

He was safe now.   He knew that the watch
was not likely to come to the superstructure for
the next hour at least.   The fellow had stumbled over a chain.   The sound, faint and far
away as it had been, caught Dan's ear instantly, leading him to mount the superstructure for an observation.

"Everything secure above there?" demanded
the officer of the deck.

"Aye, aye, sir."

"I thought perhaps you heard something,
from the way you went up."

"I thought so, too, sir, but I must have been
mistaken.   I saw no one."

Reaching the side of the ship the figure hesitated a moment, then quickly climbed through
the rail.   He was just opposite the lower boom,
the long, strong pole along which the sailors
step to get down into the small boats.

Trailing from a long rope at the end of the
lower boat rode the ship's dinghy, where she
had been left for the night, as had other boats
on the opposite or starboard side.

"Now a second figure seemed to rise directly
out of the deck, and an instant later it too had

crept out on the lower boom. The men on the quarter-deck could not see forward to the lower boom without leaning out over the ship's rail, so the two men were unobserved.

Reaching the end of the boom, the men quickly let themselves down the Jacob's ladder, dropping noiselessly into the dinghy. They had some little trouble in casting the boat off, it having been made doubly secure for the night.

Unluckily one of them dropped an oar, which fell to the bottom of the boat with a loud clatter.

"What's that?" demanded the officer of the deck sharply.

"It sounded like an oar in a small boat, sir," answered Dan, making for the topside, which, he reached in a few swift bounds.

"Something going on down there, sir."

"Where away?"

"Just aft of the port boom, sir."

"Can you see the dinghy?"

"Aye, aye, sir. Just make her out."

"Is she all right?"

"She looks to be, sir. I can't quite tell from here. I'll get over that way; I'll go further forward, sir, and let you know. I see two dinghies now. The port and starboard dinghies are moored to the port boom, sir."

"Watch them while I turn out the guard."

"The dinghy is moving, sir. I think there is some one in her."

"Dinghy, there, ahoy!" bellowed the officer of the deck.

There was no reply from the men in the dinghy, who, by this time, were making more frantic efforts to free themselves.

"Dinghy, there!" shouted Dan. "What are you doing down there?"

Dan's hail, like that of the midshipman, met with no response.

"Lay forward, anchor watch!" shouted the officer of the deck.

A quartermaster came running to the quarter-deck.

"Lower away the first whaleboat. Turn out your men in a hurry. Boatswain's mate!"

"Aye, aye, sir," bellowed a deep voice somewhere down one of the corridors leading off from the quarter-deck.

"Turn out the coxswain of the second whaleboat. Look alive, everybody."

"Aye, aye, sir," chorused several voices.

"Anchor watch!"

"Aye, aye, sir."

"What are they doing?"

"Casting off, I think, sir."

"How many men?"

"Two, I think, sir."

The officer of the deck shouted a warning to the men and ordered them to return instantly to the ship; and then, addressing Dan, he shouted:

"Stop them, if you can!"

"Aye, aye, sir."

Dan's raincoat and hat were off in a twinkling. These dropped one by one to the deck, as he sped along, bounding over obstructions that he did not even see, so familiar was he with the course he was following.

"They're rowing away, sir. I'll get them," shouted the Battleship Boy confidently.

He darted out on the lower boom, grasping the life line strung along its length for protection to the sailors passing over the boom.

"Boat ahoy!" cried Dan.

The men bent to their oars; that is, one of them did, for there is but one pair of oars in a dinghy.

"It'll be the worse for you men, down there, if you try to get away. The whaleboats are being turned out to go for you, and I'm after you myself."

His warning had no effect, unless it were to hasten the work of the man at the oars. In his excitement the fellow let an oar slip from its fastening, keeling him over on his back in the boat. A muttered exclamation reached the boy on the boom.

Without an instant's hesitation Dan crouched down on the boom, letting himself down until he hung suspended over the sea by his hands.

For a brief instant he peered down into the sea some thirty feet below him, taking mental measurement of the distance, figuring just how near he would come to hitting the dinghy were he to let himself go.

"I'll chance it," he muttered. "It's my duty to try. I am under orders to stop them, and stop them I will!"

The Battleship Boy let go.

His body shot downward, striking the water with a splash that was heard far back on the quarter-deck.

CHAPTER XIII

"MAN overboard, off the port boom!"
"Stand by the falls. Whaleboat number one!" cried the officer of the deck.

"What's this, what's this?" shouted the captain, running to the deck in his pajamas.

"Two men leaving ship in the port dinghy, sir," answered the officer of the deck.

"Step lively there, lads. What does all this mean, Mr. Officer of the deck?"

"I don't know, sir. The anchor watch discovered that there was something wrong. He's gone after them, sir."

By this time the captain was leaning over the port rail, training his night glasses on the dark sea.

"I make them out. Who is the anchor watch?"

"Seaman Davis, sir."

"You say the lad went after them?"

"Yes, sir, so it seems."

"How?"

"He must have gone over the side. for someone just called man overboard."

"The boy will be drowned! Have you ordered any one after him?"

"Yes, sir."

"Hurry, lads. The man may be drowning."

Meantime, Dan was doing his best to over-
take the fugitives. The moment he struck the
water he threw out his hands to check his
descent. This prevented his going under very
far. He shot up, and, shaking the water from
nose and eyes, struck out for the dinghy that
was still moored to the port boom.

He was clambering into the boat within the
next minute. His knife, attached to the knife
lanyard, was in his hands almost the instant
he pulled himself into the boat. One swift
stroke severed the line that held the dinghy to
the boom.

Dan sprang to the oars; throwing them into
place in the locks, he sent the little boat through
the water with long, swift strokes.

"Dinghy number two, there!" shouted a
voice from the deck.

"Aye, aye, sir," answered Dan.

"You all right?"

"Yes, sir."

"Better come back. The whaleboats will
overhaul the other dinghy."

"The whaleboats are on the other side of
the ship. By the time they get around here

the men will be out of sight. I'm under orders to get them, sir,'' answered the plucky lad, putting more force into his strokes.

His frail little boat cut the water with a swish and a splash, as the swells slapped its sides, sending showers of spray over him.

Dan now and then turned in his seat, to get the location of the other boat. He could but faintly make it out in the gloom of the night. He was unable to say, as yet, whether he were gaining on the fugitives or not. If he were gaining, it was but slowly.

The whaleboats had not yet rounded the bow of the ''Long Island.'' It seemed to take the boat crews a long time to launch the boats. The captain thought so too, for he was now shouting out his orders with explosive force, having taken command of the operations himself.

''Have an officer go in that boat,'' he commanded. ''Here, ensign,'' as an officer came up from below on the run, ''take charge of those two boats. If you don't make haste there you'll lose the dinghies and the men. Remember, one man is out there in a little boat chasing two, perhaps, desperate characters.''

''Shall we hail Seaman Davis, and order him back to ship?'' asked the executive officer.

''That boy would not hear us, even if we were

to blow the siren for him. He is obeying orders, Coates. He'll do what he was sent to do, no matter what the cost to himself. But the whale-boats should catch up with him in time to be on hand if he comes up with the others. I let him go on because, in that way, we shall keep track of the other boat. If he does that he will be doing his full duty.''

Dan was keeping the other dinghy in sight very well, indeed. He was doing more than that, he was gaining rapidly now. He could hear the splash of the oars in the other boat. The lad smiled grimly, for he knew that the others were rowing badly, perhaps because they were excited. Dan himself was an expert oars-man and every stroke in the race was made to tell.

''Dinghy ahoy, there!'' he called when within hailing distance.

The fleeing men made no reply to his hail.

''They are bound to get away. I wonder what it means? It may be that some one has been on board from the shore to steal. No; that cannot be it. It must be men from the ship, for they took a ship's boat. I'll bet they are deserters.''

He was now within a boat's length of the other dinghy, directly in its wake. Observing this, the Battleship Boy swung out a little, so as to come alongside of the other boat with several feet of water between the two boats.

"Halt!" he commanded. "You're caught. I demand that you surrender and cease rowing."

"No surrender. You go back if you know what is good for you."

The voice sounded strangely familiar to Dan Davis.

"I know you!" he shouted exultingly. "I know you now. You're Blackie. I'll bet that's White in the boat with you. Boys, stop rowing and go back to the ship. It's the only thing that will save you. I do not know why you have done this thing, but your punishment will be much less severe if you turn about and return at once."

A jeering laugh answered him.

"Then I shall have to take you back, and somebody is liable to get hurt in that operation, I am thinking."

The boy gave his dinghy a sudden quick turn, and with one powerful stroke sent it dashing up to within half a boat length of the other craft.

As he neared it he caught the swing of a body in the first dinghy. Dan ducked, flattening himself in his own frail craft just in time to avoid a vicious swing of the other's boat hook.

Dan Parried the Blow With the Captured Boat Hook.

The gunwales of his boat saved him from the blow.

Quick as a flash Davis grabbed the boat hook. He gave a violent, sharp pull and the boat hook was in his possession.

"So that's your game, is it? I'll show you that two can play that sort of game. You look out, or you'll get the pole over your own heads."

He drove his boat right alongside the other. At that moment Blackie straightened up with an angry exclamation. At the same time he grabbed an oar from the hands of his companion, making a vicious swing at Dan, who, by this time, was half standing in his own boat.

But Dan had been on the watch for just such villainy. He parried the blow with the captured boat hook.

"Smack, smack, smack!" boat hook and oar came together again and again. The battle waged so furiously that for the moment the lad forgot all about the other man in the boat. White was stealthily rising to his feet, watching the Battleship Boy with keen, menacing eyes.

All at once he swung his oar. Dan heard it as it cut the air, but at that instant he was powerless to dodge the blow, being busy parrying one from Black.

White's oar caught Dan on the head. The

Battleship Boy wavered for a brief instant, seeking vainly to catch his balance; then he toppled over backwards into the sea.

Fortunately for him, the blow had been a glancing one.

"Row, row!" cried Black. His companion fell to the oars. The men, as they well knew, were now in a desperate situation.

Dan twisted his body about in the water, his fingers closing over the gunwale of his own boat. The blow had dazed him, though he still had plenty of fight left in him.

He clambered back into his own boat with no little effort, for his clothes were soaked and weighed him down, this being the second wetting he had had within a very short time.

The other dinghy now had a slight start of him, but when the Hawaiians looked back a moment later, they saw Dan again in their wake.

The Battleship Boy's jaws were set. His fighting blood was up. He would give no quarter now.

"I'll get those heathens at any cost," he growled.

He had forgotten all about the whaleboats that had been sent for the men. Perhaps they had lost their quarry on the dark waters.

"I'm after you," shouted Dan. "This time

I'm going to get you, you miserable deserters!
Things like you deserve to be drowned without
the formality of court-martial. Do you surrender?"

"No."

No sooner were the words out of the Hawaiian's mouth than Dan drove his dinghy
bow-on against the other boat. So sudden and
unexpected had been the movement that the
islanders were taken wholly off their guard.
Black fell forward, nearly going into the sea,
while White, who was at the oars, lost his grip
on them for the moment.

A crunching sound accompanied the collision.
The bow of Dan's boat was crushed in the thin
planking of the other dinghy. The hurt was not
deep enough to sink the little craft, but it made
an opening through which the seas slopped per-
sistently.

Dan sought to swing his boat alongside the
other, when a sea unexpectedly threw him off.
A full minute of valuable time was thus lost.
Still Dan persisted. He was working at high
speed now.

This time he drove his boat right up beside
the other, so close that the two boats smashed
together with a force that threatened to break
in their gunwales.

Black, in the time that it took Dan to get

closer, had recovered himself and grasped an oar from his companion. Ere the Battleship Boy could ship his oars the enemy had swung an oar. It caught Dan a glancing blow on the forehead, the sharp edge of the oar cutting a deep gash there. The blood was in the lad's eyes instantly. He brushed his eyes clear with an exclamation of impatience.

The oar was raised for another blow. Davis did not stand still to wait for it to land this time. With a bound he was in the other boat. He had jumped from the seat of his own dinghy, measuring the distance well.

Black was taken by surprise. He had no time to dodge. Dan landed full upon him, the two falling to the bottom of the boat with a crash and a jolt that threatened to overturn the little craft.

For a few seconds the men struggled desperately, Black squirming and twisting in his efforts to get his hands up.

"He's trying to get his knife," was the Battleship Boy's swift conclusion. "I hate to do it, but I've got to, or they will have me in the sea."

He raised Black's head, giving it two sharp thumps against the ribs of the boat. That settled Black for the time being. The Hawaiian straightened out and lay still. But Dan had

been none too quick. White was standing over
him with raised oar ready to bring it down
at the first opportunity. He had not dared to
strike before, not being able to make out his
enemy as the two figures struggled at the bottom of the dinghy.

The instant that he saw Dan scrambling up
he brought the oar down. Dan dodged the blow
cleverly, the blade of the oar landing on the
side of Black's head, thus finishing the work
that the Battleship Boy had begun.

The two men sprang at each other at the same
instant. This time the boy found that in White
he had a far different antagonist. White met
him with a swift blow which barely grazed
Dan's head. Dan countered as best he could,
planting a blow on the Hawaiian's chest, staggering the fellow and at the same time well-
nigh upsetting the boat.

Blow after blow was struck in the rocking
boat, now and then each of the contestants landing a staggering punch on his adversary's head.

All at once Dan lost his footing and fell. As
he did so, he stretched forth a hand, and by
desperate effort succeeded in fastening his hold
upon the Hawaiian's arm.

White lost his balance and pitched forward.

Both men fell half over the side of the
dinghy with heads and shoulders in the sea.

For the next few seconds a desperate struggle followed. Dan held to his man, knowing full well that, were his adversary to get the upper hand now, it would go hard with Dan Davis.

Using their free hands, the men managed to pull themselves back into the boat.

By this time both were well-nigh exhausted. Their efforts were attended with little success compared with what they had done earlier in the battle. White was struggling to get his adversary overboard, while Dan was seeking to overcome the Hawaiian without doing him serious injury.

All at once the men stumbled over a seat. Dan fell prone upon the prostrate Black, with White on top of him. And there the gladiators lay, breathing hard, gasping for breath, half suffocated with the salt water that was dashing into their faces.

Everything about him seemed to Dan suddenly to grow blacker than before. He felt his head swimming.

"I'm going to faint," he gasped.

With one final supreme effort he threw the weight of White's body from him, and, rolling over, wrapped his arms about the Hawaiian, crushing the fellow down with all his strength.

CHAPTER XIV

A LIGHT came dancing over the long, even swells, sending up a shower of spray as it smashed into the white crests of the swells.

It was whaleboat number one from the battleship.

"Sing out!" commanded the officer in charge of the boat.

"Dinghy, ahoy!" shouted the seaman who was standing braced in the bow of the whaleboat, scanning the waters ahead.

There was no response to his hail.

The seaman put down the megaphone that he had been using, and, raising his telescope, swept the waters.

"Boat, sir, two points off the port bow," sang the lookout.

"Coxswain, lay your course two points to port."

"Aye, aye, sir."

The whaleboat headed for the speck that the lookout had made out through his glass. In a few minutes the whaleboat had drawn up alongside.

"She's empty, sir."

"Do you make out the other boat?"

"No, sir."

"I think I see her," said the officer. "Train your glass dead abeam to starboard."

"Yes, sir, that's the other dinghy. She's drifting."

"Then something has happened to those men. Lay to, men. Pull for all you're worth. They may be drowning while we are lying here. Coxswain, look alive."

"Aye, aye, sir."

The oars hit the water as one, and the heavy, sharp-pointed whaleboat sprang away, taking a long leap over the waves with every powerful stroke of the oars.

"Her side is stove in, I think, sir," announced the lookout.

The officer in charge made no reply. He was gazing at the bobbing dinghy through his night glasses.

"Steady there, coxswain. We don't want to run her down. Come up on the lee side and draw in slowly. She rides as if she were loaded. We shall find men aboard the dinghy, unless I am much mistaken."

They drew alongside slowly.

"Out boat hooks!"

The whaleboat made fast to the drifting

dinghy. No sooner had they done so than the officer leaped lightly aboard.

"Here they are. Lend a hand here, men. Be careful you don't upset her. The dinghy is half full of water."

Willing hands quickly transferred Dan Davis and the two Hawaiians to the whaleboat. Dan was half unconscious, while his two prisoners were wholly so.

"Take the dinghy in tow. Pick up the other one on your way, but be quick. Seaman Davis is wounded. I don't know how seriously, but he looks to be in pretty bad shape."

The men needed no further urging. In a few minutes they were on their way back to the ship, towing both small boats behind them.

"There's the other whaleboat, sir," announced the lookout.

"Hail them. Tell them to turn about and return to ship," directed the officer.

The lookout did so.

As they approached the side the battleship's rails were seen to be lined with officers and men. Dan, by this time, was sitting up and the prisoners were coming around slowly.

"Did you get them all?" called the executive officer.

"Yes, sir."

"Are they all right?"

"Pretty well knocked out, sir."

"Pull alongside the starboard gangway. Need any help?"

"No, sir; I think we can manage them. But we need the doctor right away. Seaman Davis is hurt."

"No, no," protested Dan. "I'm all right. I want to report. I'm not a baby, sir."

"I should say you are not."

Dan was permitted to stand up as the whaleboat drew up to the starboard gangway. Waiting until the boat rose on a swell he grasped a stanchion, swinging himself to the platform of the gangway by sheer grit, for he had little strength left. He poised on the landing planking, still clinging to the stanchion. A jackie ran down the gangway, extending a helping hand.

"Never mind me. I'm all right, shipmate," said the boy pluckily.

Directing all his strength to the task, the Battleship Boy climbed the gangway. Never before had the stairs seemed so long to him. At last he reached the quarter-deck.

"You are hurt, my lad," exclaimed the captain, starting forward. "Surgeon, here!"

Dan's face was covered with blood, while the white jacket was stained a deep crimson clear down to his duck trousers.

All at once he started forward unsteadily. He had espied the officer of the deck, the one whose command he had nearly lost his life in obeying.

"Sir, I beg to report that I have overhauled the dinghy and captured the men."

The boy came to attention, saluting stiffly, for it hurt him to raise his hand to his forehead.

"Very good, Seaman Davis."

"Take that man to the sick bay," commanded the captain. "Don't you see that he is barely able to stand on his feet? How about those other men? Are they seriously hurt?"

"I think not, sir," answered the surgeon, who had made a quick examination of the Hawaiians.

"Then give them attention. Master-at-arms, if the surgeon decides that they are fit, lock them in the brig. As soon as all hands are in condition we will have a quick examination."

The islanders proved to be in a more serious condition than had at first been supposed. Acting upon the surgeon's orders, they were taken to the sick bay, where their wounds were dressed and they were put to bed, with a guard placed over them.

Dan's wounds were washed and dressed and his head bandaged. The cut on his forehead where the sharp edge of the oar had struck it was deep and wide, the oar blade having gone clear to the bone, while the lad himself was weak from loss of blood.

"You are lucky that you did not sustain a fracture," decided the surgeon, as, with nimble fingers, he sewed the flesh together. "You will turn in and sleep here to-night."

"I can't do that, sir."

"Why not?"

"I am on the anchor watch, sir. I'm under orders."

"Anchor watch nothing; you'll remain here."

"I am sorry, sir, but I cannot do so until I am relieved at eight bells. If they do not want me on watch they will tell me so. I am all right now. I feel fine."

The surgeon grunted.

"Very well; but I shall tell the captain that you are unfit for duty. You have lost more blood than is good for you."

Dan left the sick bay, the surgeon watching his unsteady steps as the boy made his way down the dimly lighted corridor.

A group of officers were gathered on the quarter-deck discussing the exciting incidents of the evening, when the Battleship Boy made his appearance there.

"I report for duty, sir. I am ready to finish my watch, sir," he said, saluting the officer of the deck.

The officer of the deck looked the boy over, who, with bandaged head and pale face, presented a woebegone appearance.

"I thought you were ordered to the sick bay?"

"I was, sir, to have my wounds dressed."

"From your appearance I should say that was the place for you, not the quarter-deck."

At that juncture the captain strode across the deck.

"Davis, what are you doing here?" he demanded.

"Finishing my watch, sir," answered the boy, saluting.

"Did I not order you to the sick bay?"

"You did, sir, but you did not order me to stay there."

"I do so now, then. You will report at the sick bay at once, and remain there until you are released by the surgeon." The command was delivered sternly.

"Aye, aye, sir," answered the Battleship Boy, saluting.

"Boatswain's mate, order out another man to take Seaman Davis' watch until eight bells. Come here, my lad."

Dan had started away to obey the captain's command.   At that he turned, retracing his steps.

The captain laid a hand on his shoulder.

"My lad, I am proud of you. I know you would much prefer to remain on deck and do your duty as you see it. There is another side to this matter, however. Your duty just now lies in getting yourself into shape for the morrow. You are in no condition to work. You have done quite enough for one day."

"I feel perfectly well, sir."

"I know you think you do, but turn in and get a good night's rest. I shall require your services further in this matter, if you are able to get up in the morning. That will be all."

Dan saluted and walked off, but it was evident, from his hesitating steps, that he was reluctant to do so.

"That boy is all nerve," nodded the captain. "He has more pluck than any two men on this ship, and that is saying a good deal. Ord'ly, tell the surgeon I desire to speak with him when he is at leisure."

"Yes," agreed the executive officer. "Davis and his red-headed friend are both a credit to the service."

CHAPTER XV

D AN was released from the sick bay late on the following afternoon. In the evening of the same day Black and White were removed to the brig, and a marine sentry placed in front of their cells to see that they were properly looked after.

Dan wondered what would be done in their case. Being unfamiliar with forms on shipboard, he did not understand that punishments are not inflicted hastily.

On the morning of the second day, after quarters, there was a stir below decks. Dan had rejoined the crew of the seven-inch gun when he was informed by the captain's orderly that his presence would be required in the captain's quarters promptly at ten o'clock.

"I wish I were you to-day," whispered Sam.

"Why?"

" 'Cause there's going to be a court-martial —a summary court-martial!"

"What for?"

"They're going to try Black and White. How I'd like to help soak those heathens."

A few minutes before the hour named, Dan

went below. He found the corridor of the captain's office thronged with shipmates. In front of the door stood a marine sentry.

"Am I to go in?" he asked.

"Are you a witness?"

"Yes."

"I guess you may enter, then."

Dan did so. At one side of the room he espied Black and White, in charge of the master-at-arms; and the midshipman who had been officer of the deck the night the men escaped, together with two coxswains.

Dan walked to the opposite side of the room, where he leaned against a bulkhead.

The captain's dining-room table had been cleared and stood in the center of the room, four chairs having been placed around it. Presently three commissioned officers filed in, the executive officer of the ship taking his place at the head of the table as president of the court. It was his duty to swear in the judge advocate, who, in this instance, was a lieutenant. Following this the judge advocate swore in the others of the court and then proceeded to read the specifications, which were as follows:

" 'That on the 25th of August, 19—, while the United States battleship "Long Island" lay at anchor inside the Delaware Breakwater, after tattoo, when all hands had turned in for the night, save those on regular duty, among them being Ordinary Seaman Charlie Vavitao and Ordinary Seaman William Takaroa, the said men did secretly leave their billets and without permission take to one of the ship's dinghies, in which they rowed away from the ship with intent to desert. Secondly, it is charged that the said men did make a felonious assault on Seaman Daniel Davis while he was carrying out the orders of his superior officer, resulting in the seaman's disability, from which he has not yet wholly recovered.' How do you plead?''

The prisoners pleaded ''not guilty.'' All witnesses were then excluded from the room. Midshipman Carter, who had been the officer of the deck on the night in question, was called to testify. He was questioned by the judge advocate, who acted as the prosecutor and the attorney for the defence at the same time.

The midshipman related briefly all that had come under his observation. He had but little information that was of value to the court, and he so told the court.

''Seaman Davis, then, is the witness who knows the whole story?'' questioned the judge advocate.

''Yes, sir.''

"Call Seaman Daniel Davis to the witness chair."

Dan was summoned by the sentry. The boy's face was still bandaged; his face was pale and there was a livid mark across the right cheek where an oar blade had struck him.

Dan gave his name, age and date of enlistment, together with his station on shipboard.

"You were on the anchor watch on the evening of the twenty-fifth of August, were you not?"

"Yes, sir."

"State what occurred."

The witness related briefly the incidents leading up to the escape of the two ordinary seamen.

"You discovered them going over the side of the ship, did you not?"

"Yes sir."

"Did you try to stop them?"

"I did."

"On whose orders?"

"On the orders of the officer of the deck, sir."

"Midshipman Carter?"

"Yes, sir."

"State what occurred."

"I followed them, and after a time succeeded in overhauling the dinghy in which they were rowing away. I ordered them to surrender when I drew alongside. Black attempted to strike me with the boat hook, but I got it away from him. Black later hit me with an oar, at about the time I rammed them with the starboard dinghy."

"Well, what else?"

"Not much, sir. We mixed it up a little. I got Black, but I had a hard time with White. He almost got the better of me. I am not quite sure that he did not do so wholly."

Dan had related his story in a simple, straight-forward manner, without the slightest trace of bravado. He really had done a plucky thing in attempting to capture the two men in a frail boat out on the rolling waters, but he did not seem to think he had accomplished anything very remarkable.

"Did either man attempt to do more than defend himself?"

"Well, it seemed so to me, sir," answered the Battleship Boy, with a faint smile.

"Use a knife or anything of that sort?"

"Black appeared to be seeking to get at his knife. Of course I could not say for sure, sir."

"Did either man say anything?"

"Not that I can recall now, sir, except that they refused to surrender to me."

"You did not hear them say anything that

would lead you to believe that they were deserting?"

"Oh, no, sir."

"You can think of nothing else that will aid us in getting at the facts in this case?"

"No, sir. I have told you all I know about it."

"Very good; that will be all."

Black, who was believed to be the leader in the escape, was called up and given permission to relate his side of the story. He assured the court that neither he nor White had had the least intention of deserting. They had been on board for a long time. They said they had a friend not far from where the ship was lying, and they thought they could get away to go to see him and be back before morning.

Asked the name of the friend, they gave it without the least hesitation.

White also told a straightforward story.

"If you were not deserting, why did you make such a murderous assault on Seaman Davis?" demanded the judge advocate sharply.

"We get excited," answered White. "We want to get away then."

"And had you gotten away, at that time, you would not have returned to the ship, eh?"

"No, no; we come back," insisted the Hawaiian.

"Have these men ever been up on charges before?" asked the judge advocate.

"No, sir," replied the clerk of the court. "There are no marks against them. Their records are good, so far as the papers show."

"Then we will close the case here."

The court was cleared for deliberation. They found the accused men guilty of absenting themselves from the ship without leave, and also on the second count accusing them of felonious assault on Seaman Daniel Davis.

The court decided that the charge of desertion had not been fully established, and this alone saved the men from a long term of imprisonment. Perhaps they were swayed in their verdict by the fact that the government was making a strong effort in every way to win the regard of the Hawaiian Islanders. To have carried out the punishment in its extreme form might, it was thought, have served only to embitter the Hawaiian people. The punishment was severe enough as it was. The recommendations of the court were that Black and White be locked up in the brig for thirty days, with rations of bread and water, with a full ration every third day.

This peculiar sentence was on account of the regulation that forbids a prisoner on shipboard from being kept on bread and water for more than five consecutive days. By giving a full ration once in every five days the men can be kept under punishment for three months. The court also decided that both men should suffer a loss of two months' pay.

The commanding officer approved the findings of the court, after reading them over, and duly affixed his signature.

The prisoners did not know as yet what their punishment was to be. This was made known to them at muster that evening, when all hands were piped to quarters, the charges and findings being read before the ship's company.

"Men," said the captain after the executive officer had read the verdict of the court, "I am of the opinion that both of you should be dismissed from the service. The evidence, however, did not fully warrant the court in finding for that. It appears to be your first offence, but remember, this is your first enlistment also, which gives me the right to discharge you dishonorably from the service. I shall do so upon the next serious breach of discipline hereafter. You may consider that you have had a very lucky escape from long imprisonment and from dismissal as well."

"And, as for Seaman Davis, I desire to commend him thus publicly for his pluck, his faithful obedience of orders and the masterful way

in which he has carried out his orders. Such
men are a credit to the United States Navy.
They make one forget that, now and then, we
have some of the other sort among us. Davis,
you will be mentioned in my communication to
the department.''

CHAPTER XVI

"I EXPECT you'll be getting your whole head knocked off some of these days," growled Sam Hickey.

"It has not been knocked off yet," answered Dan with a laugh, "though it has had a considerable list to starboard on occasions."

"I should say it had. I'm glad those niggers are in the brig. They——"

"Don't use that word, please. I never liked it. And, besides, they are not Africans; they are Hawaiians."

"They ought to have been shot. Anyhow, all black looks the same color to me."

The lads were lounging on deck in the forecastle. It was Wednesday afternoon, when all hands ordinarily take a half holiday, except those who are on duty. The battleship "Long Island" was plowing up the waters off the coast —"coasting," they call it on shipboard. The officers on the bridge were taking sights at the ranges — light houses — with their sextants, while the young midshipmen, under the direction of the ship's navigator, were mathematically working out the ship's position.

"I never could understand why they have to go to all that trouble," said Sam.

"They are figuring out our position—they are trying to find out where we are."

"Don't we know where we are?"

"We don't. Perhaps the officers do."

"Pooh! I know where we are, and I don't have to get a sextant and a lot of other junk to tell me, either," scoffed the red-headed boy.

"Well, where are we, Mr. Smarty, if you know so much?"

"We're off Atlantic City. That's the Absecon light off the port bow. I could knock the top of it off with the seven-inch if I had half a chance."

"That may be true, Sam, but suppose there were a fog, or the lights on shore went out, or one of many things were to occur—supposing we were hundreds of miles out at sea and—well, how would you find out where you were, if you had no instruments with which to take your observations, or did not know how to use those you had?"

"Hold on; that's enough. Don't put on any more trimmings. I'd do without 'em, even if it were as bad as you say, and I'd never miss 'em, either."

"What would you do?"

"Do? I'd just keep going by the compass."

"But supposing the compass were wrong?"

"I'd keep going, just the same, till I got somewhere—till I plumped up against something solid; then I'd sing out, 'full speed astern, both engines,' just like the 'Old Man' does up there, when the man in the chains sings out 'by the mark five.' He's awful afraid the old ship will scrape over a sand bar. Between you and me it would be good for her. Why, don't you see, it would scrape the barnacles off her so she wouldn't have to go into dry dock and cost the government all that money. I know something about ships, I do."

"And what you do not know would sink all the ships in the Navy," answered Dan, emphasizing his reply by several nods of his head.

"Don't you believe it."

"Here comes the boatswain's mate. I think he is looking for us. Yes, he's coming this way. I reckon we shall have to turn out for some duty."

"I'll run and hide, then. I am not going to work this afternoon. He can't get me interested in any of his patriotic games to-day. No, siree!"

But Sam was destined to become greatly interested in the work that the boatswain's mate had come to talk with them about.

"Good afternoon, boys," he greeted them. "How is your head, Davis?"

"Oh, I had almost forgotten that I had a head," laughed Dan, instinctively laying a hand on the bandage that was bound about his wound.

"You did pretty well the other night in overhauling that boat. Have you done much rowing?"

"Oh, yes; considerable on the river at home. I have rowed in races there—small rowboat races— and so has my friend Sam."

"I thought you were pretty handy about small boats. It is a good thing for a seaman to know boats."

"I wonder what he's getting at?" muttered Sam, eyeing the boatswain's mate suspiciously. "He isn't here for any good, I am sure of that."

The boy had noted that the boatswain's mate was eyeing them closely, tilting his head to one side and squinting out of one eye as if he were sighting a big gun.

"Don't shoot," laughed Sam.

"What's that?"

"Nothing, only I thought you were getting ready to shoot, the way you were squinting at me."

"We are going to have some races ourselves in about three weeks."

"Is that so?" exclaimed Dan.

"Out here on the ocean?" demanded Sam.

"Not exactly out here, but in some bay along the coast. These races are a big thing and arouse a lot of interest."

"Whom do you race with?" asked Dan.

"With crews from the other ships. We race for silver cups and the rivalry is very keen. You have seen our racing gig, have you not. boys?"

"Oh, yes; that's so. I had forgotten about the gig. It's up on the upper deck, starboard side, isn't it?" queried Dan.

"Yes; that's the boat. She's one of the slickest boats in the service."

"Pretty heavy for racing, isn't she?" questioned Dan.

"They have to be for sea racing. You see, we frequently run into some foul weather. No paper shells for that kind of racing. It's a man's game, every inch of it," announced the boatswain's mate, Joe Harper by name.

"I should think it must be. What grand sport," breathed Dan. "How many men do you have in the boat?"

"Twelve, including the coxswain. We have some likely material on board this season."

"Who has charge of the race? Who is the captain of the crew?"

"I am. That is, I am the coxswain, and have full charge of the boat and the picking of the crew."

Sam was eyeing the boatswain's mate with new interest now. This time it was Sam Hickey who was squinting out of the corner of one eye. He was trying to figure out, in his own mind, what the boatswain's mate was getting at. As yet he had not been able to decide in his own mind.

"There's a colored gentleman in the woodpile for sure," he muttered. "He'll show his woolly head in a minute or so, or my name's not Sam Hickey."

The colored gentleman fulfilled Sam's expectations very soon after that.

"Unfortunately, two of our men have been taken away from us. I say unfortunately, though I don't exactly mean it in that way. I'm mighty glad we are rid of them, only that it makes necessary a change of plans."

"Who are they, Mr. Harper?"

"Those two islanders, Black and White. They are a fine pair of birds, but they certainly could pull an oar. Would you boys like to come up and look over the boat?"

"Indeed we should," answered Dan enthusiastically.

They made their way to the upper deck.

Two sailors had stripped the canvas from the racing gig, and were preparing to go over it with sandpaper to smooth its sides down.

"Why do you do that; to make it smoother?" asked Dan.

"That is the idea exactly," answered the boatswain's mate, patting the gig affectionately. We shall be working over this little craft for the next few weeks on every possible occasion."

"You do not have sliding seats?"

"Oh, no. It would not be advisable in this kind of a racing craft. You will observe, however, that the foot rests for the men's feet are made of old shoes. They slip their feet into these, which gives them a great purchase. They can release their feet at any instant, should we get upset in a heavy sea."

"Each man pulls one oar, of course?"

"One oar only," nodded the mate. "That is about all one healthy man could sit up and accomplish. None but the strongest and pluckiest can stand the kind of a race we run."

"How long a course do you cover?"

"Four miles. Two miles out to the stake boat and return. As I was saying, we have lost Black and White, and there are two vacancies on the crew at present."

"Yes, sir," answered Dan in an unusually respectful tone.

"Yes, sir," added the red-haired boy. "What about it?"

"Well, as I said, there are two vacancies," replied the mate, with a significant smile.

There followed a pause, during which Sam walked over to the rail, gazed off across the waters, apparently without being conscious of having seen them at all, then slowly returning to the gig, leaned up against it, gently smoothing the gunwale with his hand.

"It is considered a great honor to be a member of a racing crew, especially a winning crew, boys."

"Yes, sir; I should think it would be," agreed Dan.

"How would you lads like to try out for the crew?"

"We join the racing crew?" questioned Dan, his eyes opening wide in amazement. "W—we——"

"Yes. You and your friend may try for the places vacated by Black and White. They will, of course, be out before the races come off, but their punishment forfeits their right to row with us. I have been looking you two lads over, and I am sure you have good material in you. I know you have the pluck. You have shown that you have, both of you, on more than one occasion. What do you say?"

"What do I say?" answered Dan with glowing countenance. "I say that, if I could get on the racing crew, I should be the happiest boy in Uncle Sam's Navy."

"That's me," nodded Sam in approval of his companion's sentiments. "I knew you were up here for something. The colored gentleman is out of the woodpile."

"Say, Dan," remarked Sam as the boatswain's mate walked away, "speaking of Black and White, I've got an idea. I'll bet that fellow Black threw that seven-inch tompion overboard. I'll bet also that he's the black scoundrel who plugged your ear with a marline spike."

Dan made no reply, but walked thoughtfully away.

CHAPTER XVII

"HELLO, Dan."

Sam Hickey peered over the edge of his hammock in the early morning.

"What is it?" answered Davis sleepily.

"I wonder whether we have missed reveille."

"What's that?" Dan sat up very suddenly.

"I thought that would fetch you awake in a hurry," chuckled the red-headed boy, snuggling down under his bedclothes, one eye peering over at his companion.

"That's mean of you, to wake me up so early in the morning," grumbled Dan. "I was having such a fine sleep, too. I was dreaming——"

"I was dreaming. I'll bet I had a better dream than you did. I dreamed I was the captain of the 'Long Island,' with four gold stripes around my sleeve. Then I woke up. That was too fine a dream to sleep over very long at a time."

"Pipe down the guff," growled several voices from the depths of other hammocks. "What do you think this is—a pink tea?"

"No; it's a deck picnic," answered Sam, as

the bugle blew the reveille, summoning all hands from their hammocks. The men in the corridor with the Battleship Boys scrambled down from their hammocks in no enviable frame of mind, for Hickey had spoiled at least five minutes of their sleep, which was of no small consequence at that hour of the morning. Sam seized his clothes and ran for the shower bath, anxious to get his bath over before the men of his division got there. They were not in a pleasant frame of mind, and the boy considered it prudent to keep clear of them until they "got their eyes open," as he expressed it to himself.

The early morning work was finished up and then came breakfast. By this time the battleship was swinging along past Fire Island light. The sea was fairly calm and the sun was shining brightly.

"I wonder what we are going to do up here?" questioned a jackie, as they were at their breakfast.

"Up here? Where are we headed for?" demanded Sam. "Looks to me as if we were going to butt into a sand bank, the way the ship was headed when I came below."

"I think we are going into Fort Pond Bay," answered someone.

"Never heard of the place. Is it a pond?" asked Hickey innocently.

"Hear the landlubber talk. Yes, red-head, it's a pond; a sloppy-weather pond with the current so swift at times that if you were to go swimming in it, you'd want your port and starboard anchors out all the time."

"What are we going to do in the pond?"

"The Old Man hasn't taken me into his confidence yet," scoffed a sailor. "I am expecting to hear from him most any time now."

"Ordering you to appear at mast court, eh?" questioned Sam maliciously.

"That'll be about all for you, red-head."

"Better look out or Dynamite will be mixing it up with you," warned another. "Won't you, Dynamite?" nodding at Dan.

"I think I have had all the mixing-up that I want," answered Davis, with a short laugh. "If you don't believe it, just look at this bandage on my head."

"Yes, Dynamite's a sore head," suggested a shipmate. "I'd be willing to trade heads with you, if what's in yours could go with it."

At this there was a laugh all around the table. Dan blushed. He did not like these broad compliments. But, to Dan Davis' credit, be it said that, instead of making him conceited, they served quite the opposite purpose. They made him the more determined to merit the good things that were said of him.

"Torpedo practice to-day," announced a sailor, coming in at that juncture from his watch on deck.

"What range?" asked some one.

"I hear it is a four-thousand-yard range."

"That will give us all a chance to go out for a row."

"For what?" questioned Sam.

"For the exercise, red-head. We jackies never have anything to do, you know, so they have to send us out for a row, now and then."

"We don't have to row in a common whale-boat or a cutter. We've got something better in which to row," retorted Hickey.

"Got something better?"

"Yes."

"Maybe you're going to run the captain's motor boat."

"No; not yet. Maybe we'll be doing that later. Just now we're going to content ourselves with the gig."

"The gig?"

"Sure thing."

"What are you talking about?"

"I'm talking about the racing gig. Didn't you know Dan and myself were members of the racing crew now?"

"No; I didn't know anything of the sort.

You kids on the crew? That's a joke. If we fellows who have been in the service a year or two get on the crew we think we're lucky.''

''Is that right, Davis?'' spoke up one of the men further down the table.

''Partly Bob. We have been chosen for a try-out. We may make such a miserable failure of it that they will put us out of the boat after the first practice spin.''

''I'm not so sure about the red-head, but I'll risk your making a mess of anything that you try,'' answered the jackie addressed as Bob. ''I won't say you're lucky, for the good things generally go to them that deserve them,'' continued the sailor wisely. ''Leastwise, that's been my observation. I notice not many of them have ever come my way, though. What oars are you going to pull?''

''I can't say, Bob. That depends upon Mr. Harper.''

Envious glances were directed upon the Battleship Boys from all parts of the mess.

''I know how they happened to get in for a try-out,'' announced a member of the mess. ''Black and White were to row in the crew. Instead, they'll be holding down the deck of the brig for the next thirty days.''

''I was in there once,'' said Sam, with a grin that brought a shout of laughter.

"A fellow doesn't know what the sailor's life is like unless he gets in the brig."

"I think I should be satisfied without knowing, then," answered Dan. "I came pretty close to it once. That was enough for me."

By the time the jackies had finished their breakfast the "Long Island" was plowing into Fort Pond Bay, and an hour later her starboard anchor was let go. The ship's prow swung into the tide. The decks were thronged with sailors cleaning ship, while others were getting the small boats ready for the work of the day. It was a busy scene, one in which the Battleship Boys evinced the keenest interest, for they had never seen torpedo practice before. Dan had some knowledge of the operation of these weapons of modern warfare, but he was anxious to see the torpedoes fired.

First, the two steamers were swung out and lowered to the water, where they were made secure to the lower booms. The captain's motor boat came next. Two officers went off in her to place the target for the torpedo practice. This was nothing more than a bamboo fish pole with a red flag secured to it.

The target was planted in a shallow place in the bay off near the shore of Gardiner's Island, after they had measured off the course, a distance of four thousand yards from the ship. It was not intended that the torpedoes should hit the target, which was placed merely as a guide for the ordnance officer to fire at. Coming within a hundred feet of it, either way, would be considered pretty good shooting.

In the meantime the torpedo officer was far down in the hold of the ship, in the torpedo room, getting ready the huge, fish-like monsters for the flight they were soon to take. There were six of the deadly instruments of warfare down there. Dan would have liked to go below to see how the torpedoes were fired by compressed air, but his duties would not permit him to do so.

"Seaman Hickey and Davis report for signal duty!" called a boatswain's mate.

"That's us," nodded Dan. "I guess we are going out. That will be fine."

"Man the small boats and patrol the torpedo course," commanded an officer from the bridge.

"Davis, you will go out with the motor boat. Hickey, remain on board for signal duty here. We will put some of your class in the small boats, and distribute them along the course," ordered a quartermaster.

Dan's class in wig-wag work had made marvelous progress. They were now nearly as proficient in signal work as had been the regular signal corps, who were working on one of the other ships some five miles to the northeast from where the "Long Island" lay. None of Dan's men had worked at such long range before. He was glad, therefore, that he had been assigned to go out on the range, for he could keep a watchful eye on his men. He had perfect confidence in Sam. The station Hickey had was very important, for he was to receive messages and to send messages to all the small boats of the fleet.

"Now, all small boats keep clear of the torpedo course, so that none of you get hit. Don't fall in too soon after the torpedo goes by. We want the course kept clear so that we can follow it with our glasses. Take your places on the range."

"The two steamers whistled shrilly, as, with a procession of small boats in tow, they started out over the course.

"Hickey, take your place abaft of the bridge, within hailing distance of the commanding officer," ordered the quartermaster.

Sam stationed himself by the side of the box where the signal flags were kept, and, leaning against it, focused his spyglass on the rapidly receding small boats.

"Up starboard anchor!" commanded the executive officer.

Anchor chains rattled as the huge anchor was slowly raised from the sandy bottom of the bay.

The torpedoes were to be fired while the ship was under full speed.

"Once over the course, then fire on the return," ordered the captain. "Port, fire first."

"Aye, aye, sir."

The battleship completed her course at right angles to the course over which the torpedo was to be fired, then swung about.

"Full speed ahead, both engines. Raise the red flag."

The firing signal was hoisted to the peak.

"Are you ready, Mr. Ordnance Officer?"

"All ready, sir."

"Sound a long blast on the siren."

The weird voice of the siren shrieked its warning over the waters, while the prow of the battleship was rolling up a great white wave as the ship raced along at full speed.

"Fire!" came the quick word of command.

The ordnance officer pressed a button, his eyes on the target.

A dull, muffled explosion followed.

CHAPTER XVIII

HARD AND FAST AGROUND

"WOW!"

Sam, who had climbed to the top of the signal box for a better view of sea, was so startled that he lost his footing in leaping to one side.

"Look out below!" he howled. "I'm coming!"

"Gangway!" cried half a dozen sailors at once, as, with quick intuition, they discovered what was occurring.

Hickey, in attempting to right himself, had plunged head foremost from the signal box. In his descent he caught a signal halyard. He bounded up into the air like a tight-rope walker. The next instant he struck a chain that had been rigged as a railing on the companionway to the lower bridge.

"Look out below!" bellowed a voice. "Torpedo coming your way."

Sam balanced, for one awful second, on the companionway chain, then pitched downward through the open hatchway. He disappeared in the direction of the gun deck. From the commotion below it was evident to those on the lower bridge that he had reached his destination.

"What's all that racket?" demanded the captain, looking aft from the navigator's bridge.

"Signalman fell off, sir."

"Fell off where?"

"Off the signal box, sir."

"Where is he?"

"I think the gun deck stopped him, sir."

"Get another man up there to attend to the signaling. We cannot bother with such clumsy lubbers."

"No other signalmen on board, sir."

The captain uttered an exclamation of impatience.

"Find out if he is hurt. Watch that torpedo, Mr. Coates."

"We're watching it, sir. It is following a very straight course."

For a few seconds after leaving the torpedo tube, far below the surface of the water, the torpedo wavered as if uncertain what course it should follow.

All at once it straightened out and darted away off toward Gardiner's Island, where the target could be faintly made out through the officer's powerful glasses. The gyroscope, with which all torpedoes are equipped, caused the projectile to right itself. At its rear end might be seen, in that brief glance, a propeller whirling so rapidly as to cause the water to boil. the propeller being operated by a compressed-air engine within the shell of the torpedo itself.

After righting itself the torpedo dived under the water several feet, but its course could be followed by the foam it left in its path.

One of the dinghies, far out, lay too close to the course, the captain thought.

"Signalman—where's that signalman?" he shouted.

"He's coming, sir."

Hickey's red head appeared through the open hatchway, followed by the body of the limping Sam.

"Get on your station!" commanded the captain. "What's the matter with you?"

"I got shot off the signal box, sir."

"Shot off the signal box!" grumbled the commanding officer, in a tone of disgust. "Are you able to use the flag?"

"Yes, sir."

"Then signal that dinghy that they are in the path of the torpedo."

By the time Hickey had clambered clumsily to the signal box again, he was too late to be of service. Fortunately the men in the dinghy had seen the torpedo just in time. A quick

pull at the oars had turned the boat in such a
way that the projectile shot past with only a
few feet to spare.

"She's heading very straight, sir," the executive officer informed his superior.

"Yes; that's a fine run. But it isn't the fault
of our signalman that the torpedo didn't run
down the dinghy. Hickey, that was about the
worst performance of its kind that I ever saw.
See that you do not let it happen again. If
you do, I shall take you off signal work entirely."

"Aye, aye, sir," answered the Battleship
Boy, whose face was now redder than the
shock of fiery hair that was standing straight
up on his head.

"I'll show him," muttered Sam. "I'm a
clumsy lummox, but I know my business just
as well as he does his. Wait till I get a chance
to wiggle this flag! I'll make those fellows out
in the small boats think they're getting struck
by lightning. I'll——"

"Ask them if they can see the torpedo,"
broke in the voice of the captain.

Sam set his flag dancing. The moment he
began to work with it all his nervousness left
him. The red-headed boy was himself again.

"Steamer number one says they are after it,
sir."

"Do they know where it is?"

"Yes, sir; they have it located."

"Did you see the way that man Hickey handled the signal flag, Coates?"

"Yes, sir; I observed him."

"The boy is all right, in spite of his clumsiness. Can you make out the torpedo, Coates?"

"No; but I see the whaleboat putting off for it. The water there is evidently too shallow for the steamer to get in."

Sam's glass was at his eye, as he balanced himself lightly on the iron railing surrounding the signal box.

"Whaleboat number one signals that they have the torpedo, sir," sang out Sam Hickey.

"Very good. You will fire the starboard torpedo next, will you not?" asked the captain of the ordnance officer.

"Yes, sir, as soon as the men get that one on board."

The whaleboat made fast a rope to the torpedo, and then the steamer, taking the smaller boat in tow, headed for the ship, towing the monster in their wake. Reaching the ship, the torpedo was hauled aboard with a derrick and placed on the deck, to be taken apart and shipped back to the torpedo room below.

It had made a splendid flight, and all hands

were pleased with the first shot. It had been fired exactly as it would be in war time, except that it carried no explosive on the practice flight.

Dan, out on the water, was now improving his opportunity to put his signal corps through a series of practice messages. He was drilling the men of the signal corps in quick reading. First he would wig-wag a message to the fleet of small boats; then they would repeat it back to him as fast as they were able to operate the flags.

"They're signaling out there, sir," said the executive officer to the captain.

"Signalman, attention! Attend to your business."

Hickey looked up to the bridge in surprise.

"Aye, aye, sir."

"Don't you see them signaling to you out there?" demanded the captain.

"I see them signaling, yes, sir. I've been watching them for the past ten minutes, sir."

"What do they want?"

"Nothing, sir."

"Then what are they wig-wagging for?"

"Seaman Davis is drilling the squad, sir."

"Oh!"

The captain turned on his heel, giving the boy a view of his broad back.

"Mebby that one didn't land under the belt!" chuckled the red-headed Battleship Boy. "I guess I know my business, I do."

The ordnance officer announced that he was ready for another shot.

"Very well; we will get under way," announced the captain, the ship having laid to while the torpedo was being shipped aboard. "Pull over pretty close to that shore there before you swing. Chains, there!"

"Aye, aye, sir," answered the men in the chains, the little platform from which the lead is cast to determine the depth of water under the ship.

"How much water have you?"

The leadsman made a cast.

"By the mark, ten," he called in a sing-song voice.

"Keep it going."

The ship was slowly drawing near a high, sandy bluff.

"By the mark, seven."

"Slow down both engines," commanded the captain. "Give us another sounding."

"By the deep, six. . . . And a quarter, five."

"Seaman Davis signaling, sir," called Sam Hickey.

"What does he say?"

"Begging the captain's pardon, when he went

out on the range he crossed your present
course. He says there is shoal water less than
a fathom deep three ship's lengths ahead of
you, sir."

"How's your lead?" thundered the captain, turning to the men in the chains below
him.

"Quarter less ten," was the answer.

"That is plenty of water. No cause for alarm
there. Tell the engineer to go ahead."

The "Long Island" took a bone in her teeth
at once, and began forging ahead.

"Signals again, sir."

"What is it?"

"Signalman wig-wags that there is a deep
hole about where you are now. On the other
side of it is shoal water."

"Back both engines, full speed!" commanded
the captain with almost explosive force. "Keep
casting your lead! Tell me when she begins
to go astern."

"Aye, aye, sir."

"Do you know of any shoal in here, Lieutenant Douglas?" questioned the captain of the
navigator.

"No, sir; there is nothing on the chart to
show it. I guess the boy is in error."

"If so, it is the first time I ever knew him to
be. Ah! What's that?"

There came a slight jolt, then a steadying of the ship.

"She's stopped, sir," called the man with the lead. "And a half, two."

"Is she backing?" The captain's voice showed deep concern.

"No, sir. She's aground, sir."

CHAPTER XIX

A TRYING MOMENT

"KEEP those engines going full speed astern!"

There was an anxious look on the face of the commanding officer of the battleship "Long Island," for it is a serious matter to run a ship of the Navy aground.

Fortunately, however, owing to Dan Davis' timely warning, the ship had drifted very slowly on the sand bar. Had it not been for that warning the battleship would have dashed full speed into the shoal water, where she would have stuck fast for many a day, even if she did not in the end prove a total loss.

"We seem to be fast and hard, sir," announced the executive officer.

"I am afraid we are, Coates. It's too bad. How's the tide?"

"About at the turn now, sir."

"Is she making any headway astern?"

"I'll ascertain, sir. Chains, there!"

"Aye, aye, sir."

"Is she going astern any?"

"She is standing still, sir. She hasn't moved."

"Keep your lead line out. Sing out the instant the ship begins to go astern," ordered the captain.

"Aye, aye, sir."

"I'm afraid she is swinging to port, sir," announced the executive.

The captain took a shore bearing and glanced along his ship toward the stern.

"Yes, this won't do at all. We'll be on the shoal broadside in a moment. Put out the starboard stern anchor. Draw her up tight. Be quick about it!"

A splash far aft told them that the anchor had gone overboard.

"Is she holding, Coates?"

"I think so, sir."

"Watch her. When the tide turns she may shift the other way, but I think that, by drawing the anchor chains taut, we can hold the ship were she is now."

"I do not think she is very far on. We ought to float at high tide, sir."

"Yes; we should, but you cannot always tell. This is too bad, though we did all we could. I hope this mishap has not injured her in any way."

"I do not see how that could be possible, sir. It is soft ground into which she has poked her nose."

"Yes; I could tell that by the way she went aground. Sandy bottom. Signalman!"

"Aye, aye, sir."

"Send a general recall to the boats. No need to keep them out there any longer. Besides, we shall need the boats here. Boatswain's mate!"

"Aye, aye, sir."

"Have the divers made ready to go down."

"Had we not best stop the engines now, sir?" asked the executive.

"No; keep them going. But watch her closely. In case they pull her off we shall have to be careful that we do not back into the anchor chain and foul the propellers."

"Very good, sir."

"Are the boats returning, signalman?"

"Yes, sir; they are all returning, sir."

The noon hour had arrived, and the crew was piped down to mess just as if nothing out of the ordinary had occurred. As the captain's motor boat drew alongside the captain called over to the boat to pull up by the starboard gangway. In a few moments he joined the boat there and boarded her.

"Run up under the bow of the ship," he commanded.

A few revolutions of the propeller brought them to the spot indicated.

"Is this the place you signaled about, Davis?" he demanded sharply.

"Yes, sir."

The bottom, shining and white, lay in plain sight. One had only to glance over the side of the motor boat to see it.

"Pass a lead line over the side."

A line was dropped to them and at the captain's command Dan Davis took a sounding.

"What do you make it?"

"By the deep, one, sir."

"As you signaled."

"Yes, sir."

"A close guess. You have a sharp eye, Davis."

The captain peered down. He could, by getting between the sun and the bow of the ship, look down to where the prow of the battleship disappeared in the white sand on the bottom of the bay.

"Do you want the divers over, sir?" called the executive officer.

"I think not, just now. It will be useless until we get her nose out of the sand. They cannot tell us any more than we know now."

The motor boat then made a tour of the ship, the captain surveying her from all points of view. The "Long Island" appeared to be resting easily, and the sea was comparatively smooth. A glance at the skies told the commanding officer that good weather might reasonably be expected for the rest of the day.

"Return to the starboard gangway," he commanded tersely.

The captain forgot to go to his luncheon that day. He paced the quarter-deck, watching the weather, receiving frequent reports from the forward end of the ship and having frequent tests made to determine the state of the tide.

The afternoon was well along before the welcome intelligence was brought to him that the tide was flowing strong and would be high within the next thirty minutes.

"Tell the engineer to stand by to go astern full speed," he said. "All hands not on necessary duty will gather on the quarter-deck, so that we may get all the weight possible aft. Pipe all hands aft, Mr. Coates."

The boatswain's whistle trilled here and there, and was finally lost in the depths of the ship. Soon the sailors began marching to the quarter-deck until that part of the ship was packed with them.

The captain, with his executive officer, went forward to the bridge.

"I think we had better try it now, Coates," he said. "Give orders to have the anchor shipped."

"Stand by the starboard anchor," commanded the executive.

A few minutes of waiting followed.

"Ship the starboard anchor!"

"Signal the engineer to send both engines full speed astern," ordered the captain.

The bridge telegraph clanked noisily, then a quiver ran through the ship. The commanding officer stood stolidly awaiting the result. It was an anxious moment for him, meaning perhaps the loss of his command, were he to fail to get his ship off the shoal on which it was grounded. But he was calm and self-possessed.

For a full moment the screws churned the water, turning it into a sea of suds astern of the battleship.

"Chains, there!"

"Aye, aye, sir."

"Is she going astern yet?"

"No, sir."

Commanding and executive officer exchanged significant glances.

"It looks as if we were hard and fast, Coates."

"Give her time to get a foothold. The next couple of minutes will tell the story, sir."

The next few seconds did tell the story that they were waiting to hear in almost breathless expectancy.

A slight lurch to port occurred. The beating of the engines seemed to be suddenly subdued.

"Going—astern—sir," sang the man in the chains.

"All clear," bellowed the bow watch.

"Coates, we're off!" said the captain, lifting his cap and wiping the perspiration from his brow.

The jackies on the after deck set up a great cheer.

"Mr. Navigator, have you got this shoal down on your chart now?"

"Yes, sir."

"Please see that there is no mistake about it. Have you got the ranges marked on the chart also?"

"Yes, sir."

"Very good. We do not want this thing to happen to us again, or to any one else. We have been very lucky in getting off so easily."

"Are you going to have the bottom examined?" asked the executive.

"Yes, when we get to the other side of the bay. Quartermaster, head her east by south one half."

"East by south one half she is. On the mark, sir."

"Hold her there till you get that point of land abeam, then swing."

"Aye, aye, sir."

"Chains, there, keep the lead going."

The ship swung slowly round, then headed away on the new course, which she followed as the captain had directed. When opposite the point of land indicated a sharp turn was made, the vessel heading for the opposite side of the bay.

After half an hour the battleship had arrived at her first anchorage. At command, engines were stopped. Starboard anchor chains rattled loudly, sending up a shower of sparks as the anchor shot downward. Then the ship swung into the tide and came to rest.

"Do you wish the divers to go down now?"

"No; not until later. Have the hold examined, to see if she is leaking forward and report to me at once."

"Very good, sir," answered the executive, saluting. "Where will you be—here on the bridge?"

"No; I think I shall go to my cabin and have a good square meal. Strange to say, for the first time to-day I have an appetite."

CHAPTER XX

THE reports that the commanding officer received in his cabin were very encouraging. No water was found in the hold forward, and there was no indication that any damage had been done to the ship.

After finishing his lunch, the captain ordered the divers over to make an examination of the ship's bottom from the outside. They reported that the bottom was not even scratched by contact with the sand of the bay.

"We will discontinue torpedo practice for the day, Coates. It will be too late to do anything more. To-morrow we will go on with the work where we left off. I shall be busy the rest of the afternoon making a report to the Navy Department of the accident."

In his report the commanding officer told the full story, including the warning that Seaman Daniel Davis had wig-wagged to the ship from far out on the torpedo range.

In the early evening Dan was hunted out by the captain's orderly, who told the lad that the captain wished to see him in the former's quarters.

Dan was not sure whether he was in for a reprimand or not. But he hastened below as fast as he could.

"Good evening, lad," greeted the captain in a kindly tone.

"Good evening, sir," answered Dan.

"You discovered the shoal spot on your way out to the range to-day, did you not?"

"Yes, sir."

"How did you come to do that?"

"I try to observe everything, sir. The water there did not look like the rest of the water of the bay, so I looked over and saw the bottom."

"Exactly. Why did you not notify the ship? You had reasons for not doing so, eh?"

"Yes, sir."

"What were they?"

"In the first place, sir, it would have been presumptuous of me to have done so. In the second place, I thought that, of course, the navigator knew every inch of the bottom hereabouts."

"So did I," nodded the captain. "Your suppositions were wise. Knowing of the shoal place, you kept watch of us?"

"Yes, sir."

"How did you discover our danger from where you were?"

"I took shore sights as I went out, so that I might be able to locate the shoal if needed."

The eyes of the commanding officer gleamed with appreciation.

"You saw us heading on to it?"

"Yes, sir, I was watching you through the glass. When I saw that you were going to strike it, if you kept your course, I took the great liberty of warning you."

"Thank you, my lad. A board of inquiry will sit and pass upon the accident. That will, no doubt, be done within the next twenty-four hours. Other ships of the fleet will be in this afternoon, and the court will probably sit early to-morrow morning."

"And now, my lad," continued the captain, "I wish to express my deep appreciation for what you have done."

"I have done nothing, sir, except my duty, and I am not sure but that I have exceeded the limits of good discipline in that."

"By no means. Had you not done as you did the 'Long Island' would have driven full speed on the sand bar. She would be there still; she might have been there for many days to come; in fact, it might have meant the loss of the battleship. The Navy Department and the commanding officer of this ship owe you a heavy debt of gratitude, Seaman Davis. I can show my appreciation only by recommending you to the Department at the present moment. They possibly may show theirs in another way, and then I shall be able to do more for you."

"Thank you, sir. I am not looking for rewards. I am trying to do my duty, to serve my country and my Flag to the best of my ability."

"Davis, you are a splendid fellow," said the captain, rising and grasping the Battleship Boy by the hand impulsively. "Go on as you have been going, and there is little doubt as to what the outcome will be. Rest assured that I shall leave nothing undone that I can do, consistently with good discipline, to further your interests. I hear you have been chosen for the racing crew," added the commanding officer with a twinkle in his eyes.

"Yes, sir; that is, I am to be tried out, myself, and also my chum, Sam Hickey."

"I have no doubt that you will do well. It will be a splendid thing for you, giving you a new viewpoint from which to look upon the life of the sailor in Uncle Sam's Navy. I may have something further to say to you later on. That will be all for the present."

Dan saluted and left the captain's quarters.

The boy said nothing of what had been discussed in the captain's cabin. Not even to his own chum did he repeat a word of it.

On the following morning a board of inquiry
which had been ordered at once by the Navy
Department convened on board the "Long
Island" in full dress. The court consisted of
the captains and commanders of other ships of
the fleet.

The ship's company were in their best clothes
for the occasion. As the officers came over the
side, sailors manned the gangway, two on each
side, as befitted the rank of the officers visiting
the ship.

With this inquiry no one except the captain
and his executive officer had anything to do.
The board of inquiry assembled in the recep-
tion room at the stern of the ship below, where
they went into executive session, taking the
evidence of the captain, the executive officer,
and later the testimony of the navigator, who,
by his charts, proved that the shoal had been
indicated on none of them.

Dan was summoned to the court after the evidence had been taken. He was a little excited,
because he feared that his evidence would count
against the captain; but he entered the room
with confident, easy bearing and stood awaiting
the command of the president of the court.

Dan gave his name and rating in the service.
The officers were struck with the clean-cut face,
the intelligent eye and the steady nerve of the

young seaman. There was approval of his type
in every face there, but no one was more
proud of the Battleship Boy than was the captain.

To all the questions put to him by the board
of inquiry the lad gave quick, comprehensive
answers. He volunteered no information of his
own accord, merely answering the questions
that were asked of him. He told of having discovered the shoal water, and of measuring the
depth with his eye.

"How did you happen to discover that the
water was shoal?" questioned one of the officers.

"From the color of it, sir."

"How long have you been in the service, did
you say?"

"Nearly a year, sir."

"Did you volunteer to testify before this
court?"

"I did not, sir."

"It is at my suggestion to you that the lad
has been called here," spoke up the captain.
"He was unaware that he was to testify, until
you sent for him."

"You saw that the ship was headed directly
for the shoal?" asked one of the officers, addressing Davis.

"Yes, sir."

"And you signaled them of their danger?"

"Yes, sir."

"Could the shoal water not be seen from the bridge of the ship, do you think?"

"I was not on the bridge, sir. I could not say. From the direction of the sun I should say the whole bay looked alike, judging from my observation when I have been up there, sir."

"Very good."

The officer was seeking to draw out the Battleship Boy to serve some purpose of his own.

"Why did you not notify the ship at once of your discovery?"

"I did not feel at liberty to do so, sir. I considered that it would be an impertinence to do so."

"That will be all, Davis. You may retire."

The court of inquiry closed soon after that, and the board took the evidence into consideration, excluding all persons from the cabin, including the captain.

The whole ship's company seemed to feel a sense of depression. They did not believe their commanding officer had been at fault, but they knew that Seaman Davis had saved the ship. Envious eyes were cast at the lad during the rest of the day. Dan, however, appeared not to observe this. He was more worried than any of his fellows, feeling that perhaps had he acted upon his first impulse, and notified the ship's officers of his discovery, all this might have been avoided.

After the inquiry the board lunched with the captain. Then they took their departure from the ship with the same formality that they had boarded it. It was noticed, after they had left, that the commanding officer appeared much relieved. His face brightened considerably, and the lines of worry that had appeared there after the accident seemed to have disappeared.

"I guess the Old Man feels better," whispered Sam to his chum. "He must have got a hunch."

They did not know it, but the board had held him blameless, subject to the approval of the Navy Department.

"Don't use slang. And, besides, I do not like to hear you refer to our captain as the 'Old Man.' It is not respectful."

"Everybody calls him that."

"Well, you are not everybody. Be different, for a change."

"Everybody in the Navy calls the captain the 'Old Man.' "

"You never heard me do so, did you?"

"Well, no," admitted Sam; "but you're not the whole Navy."

"I'm a very little part of it, but I have my ideas as to what is right and wrong."

The captain was standing on deck watching the work that was going on. The boatswain's mate was seen to come aft on the superstructure.

"Harper," called the captain.

"Aye, aye, sir."

"This will be a good opportunity to get out the racing gig."

"Now, sir?"

"No; not now. This afternoon, after four o'clock. The tide will not be strong then and the weather is fine. Some of these lads are anxious to get their try-out, too," with a glance at Dan Davis and Sam Hickey, which brought a flush to the face of each of the Battleship Boys.

There was a stir among the crew as the captain made the announcement. All their hopes were centered in the trim racing gig. To their way of thinking there was not another boat in the fleet in the same class with the "Long Island's" racing gig. Half a dozen men were instantly told off to rub the boat down under the watchful eyes of Joe Harper. All the rest of the afternoon they busied themselves about the gig, until, at last, the command was given, "Get ready for practice spin."

The members of the racing crew hurried to

their quarters, and, at four o'clock sharp, appeared on deck, clad only in short trunks and shoes. Each man carried an oar, which he stood butt down on the deck in front of him.

The officers ran their eyes over the twelve muscular young men. The glances of all finally dwelt on Dan Davis and Sam Hickey and murmurs of surprise ran over the assemblage. Sam's arms were knotted with muscles, as were his back and legs. But it was Seaman Davis who, of the twelve, attracted the most attention.

Dan's muscles were not bunched like those of his companion; they were rounded in beautiful curves, symmetrical like those of a well-groomed race horse.

"No wonder Dynamite put a cauliflower ear on old Kester," laughed a shipmate.

"He's in wonderful condition," confided the captain to one of his officers. "That boy is a born athlete."

The gig was swinging over the side in a sling, being lowered by a big crane.

"Stand by," commanded the boatswain's mate, who was the coxswain of the gig.

The crew of the gig lined up at the rail.

"All over!"

They piled down the sea ladder, taking their places in the small boat.

"Toss!"   The oars were raised upright.
"Out oars!"

The oars were placed in the rowlocks.

"Cast off!"

The gig was shoved clear of the ship.

"Give way together!"

Eleven lusty sailors put their strength into
the oars and the racing gig shot away from the
side of the battleship, sending up a shower of
white spray as it plunged into a rising swell.

CHAPTER XXI

IN THE RACING GIG

S AM HICKEY had been given the place nearest to the coxswain, with Dan just behind him. Some of the others were inclined to grumble at that, for Sam was next to the stroke oar, a position of honor.

Joe Harper, however, had his own ideas. He wanted the Battleship Boys near him, so that he might watch their work more closely.

"A little quicker on the recovery, there, Hickey. That's better. Davis, you're doing well. You pull like an old-timer. Number one, there, you're lagging. Swing your body from the hips and come forward as if you were going to throw yourself on your face. That's it! Now get in time as I count. When I say one, every man have his blade in the water and begin to pull. Now, one! one! one! one! one! one! Keep it up!"

The gig danced over the water at increasing speed.

All at once Sam Hickey uttered a yell. In attempting to turn his head to wink at Dan he had turned the blade of his oar forward. Of course he caught a crab. The boat was moving so swiftly that the force of the blow that Hickey got from the oar doubled him up, knocking him clear back into Dan's lap.

"O-u-u-u-ch!" yelled Sam, holding his stomach, his face working convulsively in his effort to control himself.

"Hurt you?" questioned Dan.

"I—I think it turned me around inside."

"You lubber, what did you do that for?" demanded the coxswain.

"Wha—what did I do—it for? Do you think I did that for fun? Do you think I did it on purpose?" Sam groaned again.

"You were looking around; you weren't attending to your business."

"I was not looking around. I was just trying to look around. If I'd been looking around I wouldn't have fallen on my back, would I?"

The men had ceased rowing, at command of the coxswain. Some of them were laughing at Hickey's predicament, while others were grumbling.

"Nice kind of a lubber to put aboard the gig!" growled a voice.

"Silence!" commanded the coxswain. "I'm commanding this boat just now. Hickey, sit up there!"

Sam did so, at the same time making a wry face.

"Are you able to go on? If not, we'll return to the ship and get a man who is."

Sam straightened up instantly.

"I'm all right, sir. I'll never go fishing for
crabs in a gig again, sir."

The crew roared with laughter, but the red-
headed boy was as solemn as an owl.

Once more they fell to their oars. Hickey
redeemed himself during the rest of the practice. He caught no more crabs, but pulled a
steady, quick stroke that brought nods of approval from the coxswain.

As for Seaman Davis, he never missed a
stroke, and as the boat shot on he seemed to
pick up in strength like a powerful gasoline
motor under low speed on a steep hill. His oar
swung with the precision of a piece of auto-
matic machinery.

By this time the gig had gotten so far away
that she could be made out from the ship only
by the glasses of the officers. Finally they
rounded a point of land, and the coxswain
steered his boat into still water.

"Toss oars!" he commanded.

Eleven oars were raised upright, standing in
two even rows.

"Well done, lads. Out oars!"

The oars struck the water with a single
splash.

"I'd like to see any boat crew beat that for drill," announced the coxswain. "Lads, if you do as well when we get in an actual race as you have done to-day, barring Hickey's crab-fishing, you may not get the flag, but you will be well up toward the head of the line, and that's no joke. When in a race you should row just as if you were out for practice. Never get excited. Never mind what the other fellow is doing. The coxswain is supposed to attend to that. If he wants you to know he will tell you. Put every other thought out of your mind except your rowing. At every stroke keep your eyes on your stroke oar. We will now take a sprint, when I shall give you no commands. Rely wholly on your stroke oar."

At command the men began pulling. They did remarkably well, only two of them getting out of time during the entire run, which was a mile straight away.

"Very well done," announced the coxswain in an approving voice. "Davis, will you take the stroke-oar seat?"

"Yes, sir; if you wish."

"I want to see how you will hold the seat."

Dan and the stroke oar changed places.

"I want you all to be familiar with the work in every part of the boat. Stroke, I have no intention of displacing you permanently."

"I understand. That's all right, sir."

"How fast a stroke do you wish me to hit?" questioned Davis.

"About twenty to the minute. I thought you knew something about the game. Let's see if you can hit twenty."

The coxswain took out his watch.

"All ready. Stand by. Give way together."

Dan bent far forward, allowing just enough time to elapse before straightening his back to permit the other men to get into position. Then every oar hit the water at the same instant and the gig started away, but at a slightly lower speed than they had been rowing before.

"Minute's up. Exactly twenty strokes," announced the coxswain. "That was fine. Where did you learn how to time a boat? Were you ever in a race?"

"Not a big one, but I have watched the college crews practising. What little I know I have just picked up; that's all."

"You're a mighty good picker-up, then, that's all I've got to say about it," answered the coxswain, with a short laugh.

"The battleship is making signals, sir," spoke up Dan.

"How do you know?"

"I caught the flutter of a flag up aloft."

"No need of telescopes when you are

around," said the coxswain, placing a glass to his eyes.

"Recall for the gig is up," he said. "Get under way. Davis, you hold the stroke oar on the way back."

"How fast, sir?"

"About eighteen strokes to the minute for a time. We will increase it to twenty and so on up. Don't wear your men out before you get home, though."

"No, sir; I won't."

The men settled down to the long, leisurely stroke, which they kept up until they were within about a mile of the ship.

"Shall I hit her up?"

"Yes."

"How fast?"

"Use your judgment. Do you want to make a finish?"

"Yes, sir; it will do us all good."

"Go ahead."

From eighteen strokes to the minute Dan worked it up to thirty, but so gradually that the men did not realize how fast they were going. They were drawing near the ship.

"Now, every man of you look alive to his work," warned the coxswain. "We do not want to make an exhibition of ourselves when we get near the ship. The whole ship's crew would have the laugh on us. Row as if you were in a race. Watch your stroke oar. That's it. Settle right down and saw wood."

The boat leaped ahead. Thirty-two strokes to the minute rolled up, then thirty-five.

The white foam was shooting from the bow of the gig, while the coxswain was stooping forward, his glistening eyes fixed on the battleship. With a great burst of speed the gig dashed up, every man pulling, every back glistening, under the salt spray that covered it.

The rails were lined with jackies. They set up a great cheer as the boat drew in and the command, "Toss oars!" was given.

It had been a great practice cruise and the ship's company was filled with wild excitement and anticipation. Dan had made a wonderful sprint as the stroke oar.

CHAPTER XXII

"YOU are on the crew, you and Seaman Hickey," said the boatswain's mate later in the evening. "I think I will put you in the stroke-oar position, after all."

"The other man will be displeased, will he not?" asked Dan.

"Every man in that boat must be willing to do whatever he can to perfect our organization, to help us win the race, even if he has to jump overboard to do it."

Dan nodded his approval.

"I wouldn't jump overboard for any old race," muttered Sam. "I can get wet enough by staying on board."

Every day thereafter the racing crew went out. No change in the crew had been found necessary, and her coxswain considered that he had the best crew in the fleet.

Excitement was daily growing, as the time approached for the great gig race, when boats from all the ships of the fleet would enter the contest. A valuable silver cup was to be the trophy to be raced for. It would have a place of honor on the ship of the winning crew, where it would remain for a year and perhaps longer —remain until some other ship's racing crew should win it.

Each afternoon the gig's crew was turned out for a practice spin. The men were working better and better, pulling almost as one man. Even the ship's officers felt that they had never had a better chance to win the cup, and were proportionately elated.

A short cruise was made up to the Maine coast; then the ship returned to her former anchorage to complete the torpedo practice that had been interrupted when the battleship went aground.

The first night on the anchorage proved an exciting one. Off some four miles, behind a point of land where her cage masts could be faintly made out, lay the flagship with the admiral of the fleet on board. He had come in while the "Long Island" was off up the coast on her short cruise.

When an admiral is about it behooves the commanders of other ships to be on their guard, to keep a sharp lookout for surprises. Admirals are prone to give most unexpected orders at any time. For that reason the first night on the old anchorage saw more than one officer of the deck on duty. One was placed on the bridge and one aft on the quarter-deck.

. The ship settled down to silence at the usual hour; the seamen were in their hammocks and the officers had retired to their staterooms for a night's rest in the quiet waters of the bay.

Eight bells had just struck, midnight, when a messenger rushed down to the captain's quarters from the quarter-deck. Without waiting to knock, he called loudly, as he poked his head in through the curtained doorway.

"What is it?"

"Abandon ship, sir!"

Without an instant's hesitation the commanding officer reached up over his bed, pulling down a brass lever with a violent jerk.

Gongs began to crash all over the ship, from the stoke hole to the navigating bridge.

"Abandon ship!" bellowed boatswain's mates and masters-at-arms. "Abandon ship!" sang voices in the forecastle, the cry being taken up from lip to lip from one end to the other of the great battleship.

Men tumbled from their hammocks, and, without waiting to pull on their clothes, dashed for the open decks. From far below black-faced stokers ran up the companion ladders and burst out on the topside.

"Man the lifeboats! Everything overboard!" sang an officer through a megaphone.

The signal gongs were clanging automatically

all through the ship. They would continue to do so for full five minutes, giving no excuse for any one to be left on board. Boats and rafts were going over at a rapid rate, the great cranes swinging out the heavier boats with speed and precision. Most of the men were working coolly while others—the newer men on board—were showing signs of excitement.

A red-haired boy came dashing up to the top of the superstructure.

"What's the matter—what's the matter?" he shouted.

"Oh, the ship's on fire," answered some one.

"On fire—where?"

"Over there. She's going down. You'll have to hurry or you'll get caught in the suction. Look over the side and you'll see the fire coming right up out of the sea."

Sam Hickey dashed to the side of the ship and leaned forward to peer over. He did not know that the rope railings had come down at the first alarm in order to facilitate putting over the rafts and other deck equipment.

When Sam leaned, there was nothing to lean upon. The result was that he toppled right on over.

"Man overboard!" came the familiar cry.

"Cast the life rings."

"Look out below there. Man overboard!" roared an officer through his trumpet.

"Where away?" answered a voice from the boats down in the darkness.

"He fell over from topside," answered another.

"Who is the man?"

"Seaman Hickey."

"Find him, find him! What are you doing down there, you lazy lubbers? You stand there letting a man drown without making an effort to save him!"

"Who's drowning?" demanded a voice over the heads of the men in the small boats.

"Hickey; Seaman Hickey!"

"Pshaw! Seaman Hickey isn't drowning, and I don't believe the ship's on fire, either. What's the matter with you fellows? Whole ship's been having bad dreams, I guess."

"Who are you?"

"I'm Hickey. I guess I ought to know."

"Where are you?"

"I'm sitting on top of the steamer's awning just now, but if you wiggle around much more below there, I'll be in the foaming brine."

"Is that you, Hickey?" called an officer from the quarter-deck.

"Yes, sir."

"How did you get there?"

"Fell here, sir. I didn't jump, sir. Honest, I fell off the ship. I might have been going yet if——"

"That will do," commanded the officer in a stern voice. "Get off the steamer's hood, and be quick about it!"

Sam slid down a stanchion, causing the small steamer to careen dangerously. Two sailors grabbed him by the legs and hauled him aboard, Hickey's head and shoulders being plunged into the sea as they did so.

Sam came aboard choking, sputtering and threatening to thrash the whole steamer's crew.

"Silence in steamer number one!" roared an officer.

"Aye, aye," answered Sam.

"You shut up!" ordered the coxswain. "Do you think you are running this boat?"

"I nearly ran my head through the roof of the confounded thing," retorted Sam, wringing the water out of his red hair. "What's all this row about, anyway? I don't see any fire or anything else worth getting out of bed for at this time of night."

"Sam, is that you making all that noise?" questioned Dan Davis, from a whaleboat that had pulled alongside.

"I don't know about the noise. I'm in steamer number one, if that's what you mean."

"What happened to you?"

"I didn't change my mind this time, and I fell overboard, that's all."

"Did you fall in?"

"No, I fell on—and that's worse."

"On what?"

"I fell on top of the steamer. I was headed all right, but the steamer got in my way. I'd have made a beauty dive into the salt sea if the steamer hadn't got in the way. But what's all this ruction for?"

"It is a drill."

"A drill!" exclaimed Hickey in disgust.

"Yes."

"What kind of drill?"

"Abandoning ship."

"Pshaw, if I'd have known that I'd stayed in bed. The idea of a drill in the middle of the night, and after I've rowed half way to Europe in the racing gig. Who started this thing, anyway?"

"The admiral signaled all ships in the harbor to abandon ship. I presume all of them are taking the time, and we shall see who succeeded in getting away from their ship first."

"I'll bet I'd have broken the record if they had taken my time. That's the only way to abandon ship in a hurry."

"How's that, Hickey?" questioned a shipmate.

"Head first," answered Sam.

"Return to ship," came the command. "Be lively there, men. This counts on record, too. All boats to be hoisted aboard as they were."

The men piled over the side of the ship to the decks in fully as quick time as they had left. In a very brief time the small boats were emptied, excepting for the men who were manning them, two men in each boat to attend to making fast the falls for hoisting and riding up to the decks in the little craft.

The drill was ended without a mishap, save that which had occurred when Hickey tried to lean against the ship's rail and failed.

Lights, red, white and blue, were twinkling from the masts of the various ships at anchor in the bay, while officers on the bridge of the "Long Island" were reading them.

"Is signalman there?" called the captain from the bridge.

"Aye, aye, sir," came the response.

"Signal the flagship that the 'Long Island's' crew abandoned ship in four minutes and twenty seconds."

The signalman did so, working the keyboard of his signal apparatus—that somewhat resembled a typewriter machine—causing colored

lights to flash and twinkle far up on the forward
mast of his own ship.

" 'Good work, sir,' the admiral says."

"Ask him for the best time."

"Flagship signals that the 'Long Island' has
made a record for abandoning ship.   Five minutes best time in previous record.   To-night's
second-best record, four minutes and fifty seconds."

"Mr. Coates, will you pass the word to the
men by megaphone?" asked the captain.

"Aye, aye, sir.   Battleship crew, there!"

"Aye, aye, sir," roared a hundred or more
voices.

"The 'Long Island' beats all competitors in
abandoning ship by thirty seconds, and has
broken all previous records."

A roar went up that fairly shook the ship;
then two hundred voices were raised in song:

"Oh, say, can you see, by the dawn's early
        light,
What so proudly we hailed at the twilight's
        last gleaming?"

The strains of the inspiring song floated out
over the waters of the bay until one verse had
been sung, the officers offering no objection to
the jollification.   But, ere the men could begin

on the second verse, the bugle blared loudly, piping all hands back to hammocks. Ten minutes later the battleship was silent and the decks deserted. The "Long Island's" crew, almost to a man, was sound asleep.

CHAPTER XXIII

"ALL hands prepare for torpedo practice," was again the command on the following morning.

At least six torpedoes were to be fired that day, to complete the practice required of each ship. The "Long Island" got up steam and pulled away to a remote part of the bay, so as not to be bothered by the other ships of the fleet. In fact, every ship in the bay was doing the same thing—getting off by itself.

The same tactics were to be followed as had been used on the day when the battleship went aground; that is, firing when the ship was traveling at full speed, about seventeen knots an hour.

The red-headed boy was retained on shipboard to attend to the wig-wagging, Dan going out in the motor boat with an engineer and coxswain.

"Red flag up!" shouted Dan. "Keep clear of the course."

The ship's siren blew, and soon they saw the path made by the marine monster heading off in their direction. Dan, in the motor boat, was near the extreme end of the range.

"Better sheer off, coxswain, because you can't tell where the old torpedo is going when it gets near the end of its run. There she goes."

The torpedo took a long dive at an angle of about forty-five degrees from her course.

"Look where she's going!"

Off in the direction that the projectile was headed was a fleet of fishermen in small boats, tending to their nets, which were scattered over an area of a quarter of a mile, standing almost end to end.

"Head toward them, head toward them! We must warn them!"

The coxswain was a seaman, not a coxswain by appointment, and he did not appear to be as familiar with the work as he might have been. The regular coxswain of the motor boat was in the sick bay, though Dan did not know this.

"Torpedo heading your way! Look out for her!" he shouted with hands to mouth. "Pull out, men; pull out for your lives!"

The fishermen looked at the Battleship Boy, standing poised on the plunging bow of the motor boat, wondering if he had gone crazy.

"Pull out, I tell you! There she comes!"

The motor boat was driving ahead full speed.

"They'll be hit, sure as fate," groaned the boy. "They can't see her because they are so low in the water."

A yell from the fishermen told him that they had made sudden discovery of their peril. Dan, with his wig-wag flag, motioned to them to separate at a certain point. For a wonder they understood and laid to their oars in great haste.

All at once from the water right at the side of one of the fishing boats the torpedo emerged. It missed the boat by a matter of inches only, but the tail of the projectile hooked the keel. Like a flash the fishing boat turned over and the men were scrambling in the water.

"Drive in there, full speed!" commanded Dan.

"We'll get fouled in the fish nets."

"Never mind the nets. Those men may drown. Drive in there, I say!"

The man at the wheel did as the Battleship Boy had ordered him to.

"Now, slow down. Drift in."

A moment more and the life lines shot out, a half dozen wet and angry fishermen being hauled aboard the motor boat. The men were fighting angry.

Shaking the water from their clothes, they started for Dan with angry imprecations. Not only had they been upset, but they discovered that the truant torpedo was driving through their nets. Yells of rage from the fishermen in other boats told Dan that they, too, had discovered what was occurring.

On went the torpedo, ripping net after net. It seemed bent upon destruction, for, after passing through all the nets in its course, it turned almost squarely about and dived through the rest of the nets. Every net, with its burden of fish, was utterly destroyed.

Dan grabbed up a boat hook as he saw the rescued men meant business.

"Stand back!" he commanded. "I'll smash the first one of you who comes forward. Ahoy there, fishing boats. Come up here and take these men off, and no nonsense about it, either."

The men hesitated.

"Throw him overboard!" cried a more turbulent spirit.

"Try it, if you want to, men, but I warn you this is a government boat. If you commit an assault on board, or on one of its crew, you will be in for a long term in a federal prison. Think you want to take that chance?"

That settled it. The men realized that the young sailor was right, and their anger cooled almost at once.

"The government will pay you for all the damage done to your nets, as you well know.

Draw alongside here,'' he commanded to one
of the boats. ''Back out, coxswain. We are
drifting around into the nets.''

Dan wig-wagged to one of the whaleboats,
asking them to row in and make fast to the
torpedo, for his own boat could get in no further.
The fishermen, thinking he was signaling for
assistance, did not wait for the fishing boat
that was coming to take them off. They sprang
overboard and swam for the boat.

''You didn't have to do that,'' called Dan.
''You'll be saying next that we made you jump
overboard.''

The whaleboat made fast to the torpedo very
quickly; then one of the steamers towed the
huge projectile back to the ship, where it was
hoisted aboard.

For the next shot the motor boat took up its
station down nearer to the ship, about half way
between the end of the range and the battleship. Orders from the ship were to have the
whaleboats take positions at the end of the
course. They, being of lesser draught, could
get in closer to shore and could get the torpedo
out in case it drove into shallow water as before.

Near by lay steamer number two with twelve
men and an ensign on board. Both the motor
boat and the steamer cruised slowly about while

waiting for the red flag to go up on the signal halyard, warning them that another shot was about to be fired.

"Lay back farther," came the signal from the battleship.

"Motor boat or steamer?" wig-wagged Dan.

"Both."

"Steamer there!" called Dan.

"Aye, aye."

"Battleship orders you to lay back farther, and to keep off the course."

The steamer shifted its position, and Dan's boat pulled farther away, at the same time moving off a little more toward the shore. The two boats were now on opposite sides of the course that the torpedo was expected to travel, though one can never be sure just where these instruments of war are likely to go.

"Battleship under way," signaled Dan to the other small boats out on the field.

For a time he watched the warship that was heading for the other side of the bay. Finally the ship turned and started back, with a big, white "bone between her teeth," as the saying goes when a ship is plowing up the sea.

"Red flag going up," called the signal boy. "Wherry, there, ordered to lay to starboard of the target," he signaled to the little boat dancing on the waves half a mile away.

The small boat quickly took its position as ordered from the ship.

The siren blew a long blast, and with eyes turned toward the ship, all the boat crews pulled back to a safe distance.

"Torpedo on the way," signaled Sam Hickey from his position on the ship.

"Torpedo under way," wig-wagged Dan Davis to the other boats. "Get under way, the battleship signals," he told the little fleet.

At the same time the motor boat started along the course that the torpedo was expected to follow, the small steamer a little in the lead.

"She's running close to the surface," muttered the Battleship Boy, watching the projectile. "I can see the water spurting from her bows. She'll never complete the run."

He turned to look at the steamer. He observed that she was at right angles to the course.

"Sheer off! Sheer off!" shouted Dan. "You're right on the course. You'll be hit!"

"We're disabled. Motor boat, there!" shouted the ensign in the small steamer.

"Aye, aye, answered Dan.

"Lay over and help us out. We've thrown our propeller."

"Full speed ahead. May I take the tiller?"

The acting coxswain good-naturedly stepped

aside, Dan taking the steering wheel of the motor boat from his hands.

The lad's eyes traveled rapidly from the advancing torpedo to the steamer that was rolling on a heavy swell, her crew of more than a dozen men leaning over the side, straining their eyes to make out the torpedo.

"She's going to strike us, sir," shouted the coxswain.

"Can't help it," answered the ensign. "All hands be ready to go overboard when I give the command. Some of us will be caught. We don't know where she is going to hit us."

The officer knew that only a miracle could save some of his crew from being crushed to death when the heavy torpedo struck the little steamer. To move the men to safe parts of the boat was not possible, for it was impossible to say where the projectile would strike. Perhaps she might change her course and not hit them at all. That seemed to be the only hope now.

Turning their eyes, they saw the motor boat smashing through the sea, throwing the water high from her bows. Dan Davis was leaning well forward, one hand on the steering wheel, the other on the engine control, his eyes watching the torpedo and the steamer.

Now he would slow down ever so little, then

drive ahead at full speed, as if jockeying to cross the line in an international race.

The ensign was watching him with fascinated interest. He knew that the boy had some daring plan in mind, but what that plan was he could not understand. The officer was on the point of shouting to the Battleship Boy to turn in and push them out of the way, but he refrained.

Dan had thought of this very thing, but he knew the chances were against his being able to do so. He chose a bolder and more brilliant way of saving the boat's crew, or of trying to save them.

The engineer of the motor boat was under the hood watching the engines.

"Get out of there quick!" commanded Dan.

The engineer came tumbling out from his cramped quarters.

"What—what——" he exclaimed.

"Keep still! Don't talk to me. All hands hold fast, for something is going to happen in a minute."

At that instant the lad swung the bow of his boat about, heading it directly toward the course of the advancing torpedo.

"Look out! You'll run into her!" yelled the engineer. "Don't you see she's just under the surface. She'll be on top—there she is now!"

"Stand fast!" roared the boy.

Torpedo and motor boat were driving toward a point where they must surely meet. Now Dan threw the speed full on.

Ere any of those wide-eyed observers realized what was occurring, the crash came.

The prow of the motor boat and the nose of the torpedo met with a crash that was heard far down the line. For a brief instant, projectile and boat rose into the air like two locomotives in a head-on collision.

Dan Davis was lifted clear off his feet and hurled through the air, head first, into the sea. The motor boat settled back and began filling with water, half drowning the two stunned seamen who lay in the bottom of the boat. The torpedo, however, like some living monster of the deep, seemed to shake herself angrily, then she settled down and shot forward, barly grazing the stern of the steamer.

Dan Davis' heroic effort had deflected the torpedo slightly from its course, just enough to cause it to clear the little steamer, thus saving the lives of at least part of the crew aboard her. A life ring at the end of a rope brought Dan out of the salt water not much the worse for his thrilling experience.

"How's the motor boat?" was his first question.

"Pretty hard hit, I guess," answered the ensign. "But that doesn't matter."

The other steamer, having observed that an accident had occurred, put on all steam and hastened to the scene of the wreck. About that time some one discovered that the ship was making signals, and the ensign asked Dan if he felt able to answer them.

For answer the lad asked for a signal flag. One was placed in his hands, together with a spy glass.

"Battleship asking what the trouble is," he called.

"Tell them."

"Aye, aye, sir."

"And, while you are about it, you might tell them that Seaman Davis, by his quick wit and pluck, saved the steamer and perhaps all our lives."

"Is that a command, sir?"

"No. Only a suggestion," answered the ensign, with an indulgent smile, as he noted the boy's confusion.

"Battleship signaling for motor boat and steamer to return, sir."

"Tell them we both will have to come in in tow, then."

"Orders for second steamer to tow us in, sir."

The ensign gave the order to the other steamer.

While all this was going on a whaleboat had run alongside the motor boat and had taken off the two men who had been left on her. They were more or less dazed, but not seriously hurt. A brief examination of the motor boat's engine developed the fact that the engine had been wrenched loose from its foundation. The nose of the boat had been badly smashed.

Dan was of the opinion, however, that the damage to the boat could be repaired in a day. Things were not nearly so bad as they looked to be at first glance.

The two disabled boats, towed by the steamer, made their way slowly back to the ship.

"This torpedo practice has been a fine piece of business," Dan confided to a shipmate. "It strikes me that this will be a good time to quit, or somebody will get hurt."

"I guess you are IT, then. You'll catch it when the captain sees his motor boat," answered the other, with a laugh.

The captain's lips pursed as, through his glasses, he made out the broken bow of his boat. He said nothing until Dan and the ensign had boarded the battleship.

"Ensign, who is responsible for the condition of that boat?" he demanded.

The ensign stepped aside and held a few moments earnest conversation with the commanding officer. As he went on the stern expression on the captain's face gave place to one of admiration. He nodded his head approvingly. Those who did not understand how the motor boat had been wrecked, felt sorry for Seaman Davis. In fact, Dan was beginning to feel sorry for himself, as he realized what he had done.

"Davis, come here!" commanded the captain.

The boy approached, saluting.

"Mr. Brant has told me the story of your brilliant exploit. I congratulate you, my lad."

"I—I am sorry, sir, that I smashed your boat."

"What is the boat when compared to a human life?"

"That—that is what I thought, sir. I did not think you would feel very sorry about the boat when you knew."

"I should say not. But what about your own life? You gave no thought to that, did you?"

"N—no, sir."

"That is the way with all brave men, and that act of yours was one of the bravest I have ever seen. I want every man on board this ship to know about it—to hear the full story. Mr. Coates," beckoning to the executive officer.

"Aye, aye, sir."

"Call a general muster on the quarter-deck to-night and read my commendation of Seaman Davis' heroic conduct."

"Aye, aye, sir."

"But, Davis, I am sorry to say that your racing ambitions will not be gratified this fall."

Dan's face showed his disappointment, but he said no word.

"The first torpedo, one of the unlucky ones, fell on Boatswain's Mate Harper as it was being hoisted aboard, and broke a leg. Some one was to blame for the accident. I do not know who, but I shall know."

"Oh, that is too bad!" breathed Dan, turning away to his disappointment.

"It's all off, Sam," he said when a few minutes later he joined his chum.

"What's off?"

"The race we were to row day after to-morrow."

"On account of Joe Harper?"

"Yes, have you seen him?"

"No; I guess they won't let anybody see him to-day."

The boys went about their work for the rest of the day with downcast countenances. The entire crew was in the doldrums. All their hopes, pinned to the "Long Island's" racing crew, had been suddenly dashed. A race now seemed out of the question. There was neither laughter nor song in the forecastle that night. All hands went to bed surly and disgusted.

On the following morning the captain's orderly called Dan Davis from his gun station, with the information that the captain directed Seaman Davis to proceed to the sick bay to see Boatswain's Mate Harper.

Dan obeyed the order, wondering at its having come to him through the source it did.

"Oh, I'm so sorry, Mr. Harper," said the lad as he entered the sick bay, and the boatswain's mate extended a hand to him. "I'm sorry for the race, and I am sorry for you. It's too bad."

"Yes; I've got a bad knockout. I don't believe my leg ever will be right. I guess they will retire me, all right. But that isn't what I sent for you to talk about. I want to talk about the race."

"The race? Why, there won't be any race now—that is, so far as we are concerned. Some of the other ships will carry off the cup now."

Harper smiled wanly.

"There must be. The crew must run the race just the same."

"But it will not be possible without you."

"Perhaps there is no one on board who un-

derstands the racing game quite as well as I do.
I have run many of these gig races, Davis. But
there is one man on board in whom I have great
confidence. He has the pluck. He knows rowing. Even if he doesn't win, which could
hardly be expected of him, he'll make some of
the other fellows work for their laurels.''

Dan's eyes were glowing.

"I—I am so glad to hear you say that, Mr.
Harper. That is good news, indeed. Then we
will have the race after all?''

"Yes; the race will be run. They shall not
have an opportunity to say that the battleship
'Long Island' got cold feet at the last minute.''

"They'd better not say it before me,'' answered Dan in a low voice.

"That's the talk!''

"May I ask who the man is who will act as
coxswain of the racing gig in to-morrow's race,
sir?''

"Yes, you may. You will be surprised when
I tell you. The man who is going to run the
'Long Island's' boat is named Daniel Davis.''

"Da—Da—I—I am to be coxswain to-morrow?'' gasped the boy.

"Yes, you, Dan. And you're going to do
yourself and every man on this great ship
proud.''

Dan sat down in a chair rather suddenly.

His face was pale and his eyes seemed larger than usual.

"I—I am to race the crew?"

"You are to race the crew. I have asked that you be released from duty to-day. Go off somewhere by yourself and think it over. Get your balance; then come back here and we will talk it over."

Dan walked out of the sick bay without a word. His emotions were so great that he could not talk.

CHAPTER XXIV

THE jackies of the battleship set up a great cheer.

Coxswain Davis and the eleven men of his racing crew were lined up on the quarter-deck of the "Long Island." On the decks of a dozen other ships in the bay a similar spectacle might have been seen.

The great race for the silver cup was about to be run. But, now that Joe Harper was unable to guide the boat of the "Long Island," the other ships feared none save the racing crew of the "Georgia."

"Never mind if you don't win, Dynamite. You've got the pluck; you've got the sand. It won't be your fault. But make 'em hump. Make 'em work for what they get," shouted a jackie.

Dan smiled faintly. There was little color in his face, but no one was able to find a trace of nervousness there.

"If that boy had the experience, I should expect to see him win," confided an officer to his companion.

"I don't know. This putting green men in

a racing boat is bad business. I hear he has
put his friend Sam Hickey in as stroke oar."

"Yes."

The officer shook his head.

"All aboard," commanded Dan. The boy
had received detailed instructions from Joe
Harper; yet, for all of that, all depended upon
Dan and his crew. No one could coach them
to the winning point from a sick bed.

The men took their places in the gig. A gun
was fired from the flagship warning the crews
to start for the stake boat. As they pulled away
the sailors lined the side of the battleship, cheer-
ing until they could cheer no more. Something
in the quiet determination of Dan Davis had
filled them with hope. A practice spin, the
night before, had put Dan and his men in closer
touch. They, too, felt a confidence in the little
coxswain who never lost his head nor got excited, no matter how great the emergency.

The race was to be four miles, two miles and
a turn, starting from the scratch, the bow of
the flagship marking the starting point. The
turning buoy was just past the "Long Island."

The racing boats lined up off the flagship
where the men received their instructions from
the referee, who shouted out his orders through
a megaphone. The racers were to start on a
gun signal.

The Battleship Boy's slender figure, hunched down in the stern of the "Long Island's" gig, brought a smile to the face of many men that bright afternoon. It seemed a joke that a boy —a mere apprentice—should be given so important a post as that. Dan understood; he knew that the other crews were laughing at him.

"Lads," he said, as they were paddling around for the scratch, "they think we are some kind of joke. Let us show them that we can give, as well as take. Keep steady. There's credit enough to go all around. If we win, no one of us will have won. All of us will have. If we lose, all of us will have lost. All ready now; toss oars!"

An interval of a few seconds followed.

"Let fall! Attention! Stand by!"

Every back was bent.

"Steady, Sam. Do your prettiest."

Sam made no reply.

"Boom!"

The flagship's six-pounder belched forth the starting signal.

"Go!"

The command from the little coxswain came out like the bark of a pistol.

The racing gigs of the fleet leaped forward, driven by powerful arms and backs, the bows

of each boat rising right out of the water under
the first pull of the long oars.

Sam, at command of the coxswain, had
started in with twenty-five strokes per minute.
The other racing boats had struck a higher
pace, resulting in their forging ahead. The
"Idaho's" boat took the lead at the start.

Dan was sitting calmly in the stern of his
racing gig, his hand resting lightly on the tiller,
watching his men and at the same time keeping
his eyes roaming over the water, noting the
position of the other boats and steering his
course. He used the "Long Island" for his
mark, steering to starboard of her, for at the
distance no skipper was able to make out the
turning buoy.

"Thirty-two!"

Sam hit up the stroke.

"Hold it there steady!"

The "Long Island's" gig forged ahead a
little. They were now half way to the battleship.

"Thirty-five!"

The little boat was beginning to send a shower
of spray over the backs of the oarsmen. Other
boats were astern of them now, but four leaders
had a good start.

"Thirty-eight! Make a good showing.
We're going to pass our ship now. Give them

a run for their money. 'Idaho,' 'Georgia' and 'Connecticut' now have the lead. Take it easy, boys; don't get excited. We'll drive them out pretty soon. 'Idaho' is splashing and 'Georgia' just caught a crab.''

The gig was rapidly closing the gap that lay between it and the three boats ahead of them. The fourth one was abreast, the others, a short distance astern.

"We've got them, boys. They shot their big guns at the start. Now keep her going as if you were an old family clock.''

A roar sounded in their ears as they plunged past the battleship. The huge cage masts were white with jackies, yelling and swinging their hats, while every inch of rail on that side of the ship was occupied by officers and men. The turn was made. The "Long Island's" gig was leading the second boat by three boat lengths.

"Snap!"

The stroke oar tumbled over backwards. Sam's oar had snapped short off.

A great groan went up from the decks of the "Long Island."

"It's all off," cried an officer. "The stroke oar is broken."

"Wait! What's going on over there?"

"Jump!" shouted Coxswain Davis. "Jump, I say!"

Sam hesitated, for an instant; then the purpose of his chum dawned upon him as he rose, crouching, from his seat.

Dan gave his companion a mighty push and Sam Hickey went overboard. A life ring went soaring after him.

"Into his place, number two!"

The man who had been Joe Harper's stroke oar slipped over into the seat vacated by Sam Hickey.

Dan sprang up on the rear seat with the tiller between his legs.

"Go! One, two, three, four, five, six, seven, eight, nine, ten," he counted rapidly, to get the new stroke started in his pace.

The "Idaho" and "Connecticut" had gained a slight lead over Dan's boat in the brief delay.

Observing Coxswain Davis' remarkable act, the sailors once more set up a yell, and such a yell as it was!

A boat was quickly manned and a crew of jackies pulled to the place where the red-haired Sam was clinging lazily to the life ring that Dan had cast to him.

"He threw me overboard," complained Sam.

"That is the greatest piece of quick wit that I ever saw in my life," laughed the captain excitedly. "That boy deserves to win, but he can never do it with one man short in the boat."

Coxswain Davis had other views. He was still standing on the seat of the rocking, plunging boat, snapping out his commands to his men, and every man in that boat was thrilled with the encouragement that the little coxswain had instilled into him.

"Go it! Beef it! More steam, number four! Swing further, number eight! Hip! hip! hip! hip! hip! Hit her up! Faster, faster, I tell you! You're winning, I tell you! Drive it! Forty-five, stroke oar."

"I—I can't," gasped the stroke.

"Drive it, I tell you!" yelled Dan Davis, grabbing up the boat hook, brandishing it threateningly over the head of the stroke oar.

"Hip! hip! hip! hip!" he began sharp and quick, setting the pace for the higher speed. The stroke oar, with the perspiration running down his body, reached the stroke demanded.

"Now, hold it, or I'll bat you with the boat hook!" threatened Dan. "Hip! hip! hip! hip! Gaining on the 'Idaho.' We've passed her. Quarter of a boat length to the good. We've got to make it more, or she'll spurt us out at the finish. Hold her there. Here she comes. She's abreast. She's spurting. Hit her up to fifty. Hit it, if it kills you! You've got to win this race, if every man in the boat drops dead."

Dan was dancing about on the slender support of the stern seat, yelling like a madman, though there was not the slightest trace of excitement to be seen in his face. Those on the flagship could hear him shout and see his body moving back and forth to set the pace for the stroke oar. It was a sight that not a man who saw it ever forgot. Discipline on board the ships near by was almost forgotten. The men were shouting and yelling in their excitement.

"The "Idaho" and the "Long Island" were bow and bow. Scarcely two boat lengths separated them abeam. Dan knew they were there, but he did not look. His eyes were on his men. A slip, a mistake now, and all would be lost.

"Fifty-five for the last time. Every ounce of muscle on the oars, lads. Go it. Kill 'em! Eat 'em alive! Whoop it up! Hip! hip! hip! hip!"

The words came out with explosive force, almost with the rapidity of a Gatling gun's fire.

"Boom!" roared the flagship's six-pounder.

Two boats shot over the line with every siren in the fleet wailing its greeting to the winning crew.

The men in the "Long Island's" gig did not know they had finished.

"Cease rowing!" commanded Dan in a weak voice. His strength was well-nigh spent. The gig's crew swayed in their seats as they feathered their oars, with difficulty holding their weary bodies from going overboard. They were almost wholly spent.

"Long Island" wins by half a boat length," announced an officer from the deck of the flagship.

A signal fluttered from the peak of the flagship's signal halyard, giving the news to the rest of the fleet.

"Boom!" roared the "Long Island's" sixpounder; then her siren screeched madly.

Dan stood up and saluted the officer of the deck of the flagship.

The winning crew rowed slowly back to their own ship, after a few minutes' rest. As they approached the "Long Island" the siren let loose again. Sailors danced and yelled, throwing their caps into the air, mad with delight.

"Enough way," commanded Dan as his boat drew alongside of their ship. A group of sailors dashed down the gangway, stretching out their hands for him.

"Get the boys out first," he said, with a pale smile. "They've worked harder than I have. But the jackies would not have it that way. They hoisted Dan to their shouders. Others did the same with the rest of the crew, and as the victorious men came up over the side, the ship's band struck up "The Star Spangled Banner.'' A scene of wild excitement followed. Nothing like it had ever been seen on the quarter-deck of the battleship. Dan Davis and his crew had won what had been considered a hopeless battle; they had won the cup in the greatest race in the history of the American Navy.

The captain, with his officers, as soon as they could get near enough to do so, grasped Dan by the hand. He and Sam Hickey, and the others of the crew, were the heroes of the hour.

Davis and Hickey were called before the captain a few minutes later, in the presence of the entire ship's company.

"Lads, this has been a great day," said the commanding officer. "We are all proud of you. And this is a most appropriate time to tell you something else I have to say—to read an order from the Navy Department at Washington which directs that Seaman Daniel Davis, for meritorious conduct, in saving the battleship from wreck, be immediately advanced to the petty-officer class, with the rating of gunner's mate, first class. The same order directs that Seaman Samuel Hickey be advanced to coxswain. Lads, I congratulate you. You deserve it. Continue as you have been doing, and some day you will be on the quarter-deck."

Another deafening roar of applause greeted the announcement. The Battleship Boys had made their first real step upward. They had won their grades as petty officers. But they were only at the beginning. The ladder that they had set themselves to climb still towered high above them. They were bound to climb, however. They determined that they would not remain on a lower rung of the ladder. This was merely a beginning. Other promotions were ahead of them, promotions that were destined to come sooner than either lad dreamed. The story of these new honors, of other brave deeds, valiant efforts and stirring experiences in other climes will be told in a following volume, entitled "THE BATTLESHIP BOYS IN FOREIGN SERVICE; Or, Earning New Ratings in European Seas."

THE END.

www.ingramcontent.com/pod-product-compliance
Lightning Source LLC
Chambersburg PA
CBHW050507260626
47157CB00004B/1225